THE QUEST

THE QUEST

by Hanna Stephan

TRANSLATED BY
DAPHNE MACHIN GOODALL

Illustrated by Antony Maitland

Little, Brown and Company
BOSTON   TORONTO

LIBRARY OF CONGRESS CATALOG CARD NO. 68–15390

FIRST EDITION

First published in Germany by Fischer Verlag, Göttingen

This book was published in Great Britain
by William Heinemann, Ltd.
as *The Long Way Home*

F
Ste

Copy 1

PRINTED IN THE UNITED STATES OF AMERICA

Author's Note

This story is based on original documents relating to a child who was lost in East Prussia when the Russians entered World War II and who was traced by the Red Cross in Hamburg nine years later.

Contents

PART ONE

1

We Must Flee

PETER REISIGER was now fourteen years old, but he was sure of it only when he began to count — he had lived through so much that he had not been able to pay attention to the passing of the years.

There had been only summer and winter — summer and winter so many times, and they had been full of adventure, strange lands, strange people, danger and security. There had been places where people were crowded together, and others which were as empty as the desert. There were mountains too, which reached up to the sky, flowing rivers, seas, cities, lonely huts, monasteries and palaces. Peter had seen them all since he had started off to look for his mother.

He had been five years old when it all began; he knew this exactly because his mother had taught him to repeat his name, where he lived, and how old he was.

"What is your name?"

"Peter Reisiger."

"How old are you?"

"Five."

"Where do you live?"

"Ten Middle Road."

This lesson had accompanied him on his long journey across the world, and in the end it had helped him to find his way home. Of course, it wasn't just this bit of knowledge by itself; everywhere he had found kind people who took care of him and helped him further — because in every country there are kind people. And kindness can overcome barriers and help a child who is lost in the world to find his way home to his mother.

During the nine years Peter had forgotten what his mother looked like. When he tried to remember he thought of that last evening at home. He had been asleep and woke up because the wardrobe door creaked. The light was burning and the windows were blacked-out because of the war, and behind them was the sound of gunfire which had been going on for days. The girl with fair hair who stood in front of the wardrobe door was his mother; over one arm she carried a blue silk dress with colored flowers which she touched softly and with a sigh put back in the wardrobe. An open suitcase lay on a chair.

Peter sat up in bed. "Are we going on a trip, Mother?"

"It's possible that we shall have to leave tomorrow morning," his mother said sadly.

"How lovely!" Peter cried, but his mother came and sat down on his bed and took him in her arms.

"Don't be glad about it, Peter, because we shall be refugees then, like all the others who have come through the town and who went away over the bridge."

"Are we going in a wagon?" Peter wanted to know, and was quite glad about this idea.

"Herr Hantusch sent Clare over to say perhaps we could go by train, and that I should pack my suitcase and your rucksack." His mother stood up and there were tears in her eyes. She went to and fro while Peter watched.

"You're always afraid, Mother, and I never am — I am glad, and you're frightened."

"You're like your father," his mother answered, looking across the room to the small picture in the silver frame which stood on his father's writing table. A soldier with clear eyes and a happy mouth smiled back at her.

"Where's Father now?"

"Somewhere in the East," his mother said.

"East — West — tell me about it, Mother."

"I'll tell you later, Peter — now I have to pack," and she took things and put them in the suitcase.

"Don't forget the silk dress. Father likes that best of all."

"But we can only take a few things; the dress will have to stay behind."

"It's a pity."

"Of course!" his mother replied. "It's not easy to leave behind everything one loves."

"My rocking horse — and the train engine — my Teddy bear. . . ."

For the first time Peter had a funny feeling inside him. But the thought of a long journey was so wonderful that leaving home was nothing in comparison.

"Is the world very big, Mother?"

"Very big."

"I do want to see it — and I *am* glad."

In the middle of this joy he went to sleep. Sleep came to him as softly as the rustle of his mother's silk dress. It muffled the sound of the guns and the tinkle of broken windows, and his mother's footsteps and her soft crying.

When he awoke next morning, the sound of gunfire had come so close that one could hear the patter of bullets. The window frames rattled, the panes cracked and the whole house shook.

His mother was standing in front of the chair closing the suitcase. Suddenly the lock clicked.

"That's all," said his mother, "— if Father only knew."

Now with quick hands she packed Peter's rucksack, then she dressed him, putting on his green pullover under his red woolly jacket; on his head went the red knitted cap with the thick pompom, but she forgot to smooth down his fair hair, as she always used to do. Every so often she looked out of the windows; when the guns fired the curtains blew out. They heard footsteps, the sound of wagon wheels and excited voices.

"What's happening out there?"

"People are leaving."

"But the shovels? Men and women — and shovels and picks?"

"They have to dig trenches," his mother explained.

"In winter?" Peter thought of his little garden behind the house which lay asleep under the snow.

"They have to dig trenches around the town — so that the Russians are stopped for a little — Herr Hantusch —"

Herr Hantusch came in — he was an old man, bent double with rheumatism. He was so lame that he couldn't dig trenches.

"It's time now, Frau Reisiger," said Herr Hantusch. "Time to go. I promised your husband to look after you, and I certainly will." Herr Hantusch looked at Peter. "Now then, put your rucksack on your back and come. There's a train in the station which will take women and children. Come along — quickly!" And he was already down the stairs.

Mother said, "Run along down, Peter, but wait outside the door — do you hear? I still want —"

Peter also wanted something. He went quickly into his bedroom, flung himself on the bed and grabbed the Teddy bear, who was still asleep.

"You'll have to come too."

The world was very big — and now Peter was going to

explore it. If Mother didn't see the bear until they were outside, then she'd let him come.

As he ran downstairs the rattle of shots outside sounded like peas in a colander.

For a second all was quiet and then people began shouting in the street — and there was the sound of hurrying footsteps.

Peter stood outside the door — the road was nearly empty. In the distance a yellow tank rolled around a corner and there was Herr Hantusch running more quickly than Peter had ever seen. He turned and waved: "Hurry! Hurry up!" Then he disappeared.

Peter had never seen the road look so wide and friendly. A band of sunshine lay across the snow on one side, and on the other lay the blue shadows of the houses. A cat jumped out from a cellar and came springing toward Peter, weaving itself around his feet. Peter bent down and the bear growled.

"Pussy, pussy." He began to run after her; this was a fine hunt. The bear growled again and the rucksack bounced. The cat slipped through the hedge; she seemed to wait for Peter under the whitethorn bush, but every time he tried to catch her she sprang away from him.

"We'll get her somehow, Bear," said Peter. "It's Herr Hantusch's cat and we must take her back." They had to be quick because Mother was waiting, but first they had to get the cat.

Before Peter noticed, the hedge had ended. And with

one leap the cat had disappeared over a garden gate.
Then a thrush began to whistle. It hopped off across the
snow toward the meadows and Peter and his bear followed, now chasing the thrush. It hopped, then fluttered
across the meadow and stopped on top of a frozen mole-
hill where it began whistling again; like a little flame Peter's red cap bobbed along behind it. Then the thrush
gave a loud peep, opened its wings and flew away.

Peter stood in the middle of the meadow and looked
around. The sky was a lovely pale blue and the snow glistened under the sun. The world was huge and lovely and
he was in the middle of it all. It was so still he could even
hear himself breathe. How happy he was! But he must
run home because Mother would be waiting, and he
wanted to tell her about Herr Hantusch's cat.

2

Peter and the Strange Father

———————————————

SUDDENLY a bang broke the stillness, a wild clatter and a loud whistling. It came from across the meadow over Peter's head and landed in the hedge which bounded the gardens on the outskirts of the town. On the other side of the meadow heads wearing fur caps began to appear above the snow. Frightened, he turned around, only to see men appearing from under the hedge — men in uniform with weapons in their hands, which they used to shoot back across the meadow. Some of them must have seen Peter, because they stopped shouting and called to him, but the noise from the other side was so loud he could not understand them.

There he stood quite plainly in the snow in his red woolly jacket and his red cap. So this was what war was! He was too small to understand that the rifles and guns which the men held had been made to kill people. He didn't know anything about dying. So he was not a bit upset that he had managed to see this for himself. The journey had begun well!

The men across the meadow had seen him too, and

they also called to him, in strange words which he had
never heard before.

One of them rose, breast-high, out of the snow and
waved to him. But he disappeared quickly, for a bullet
came from the direction of the hedge, smacked down in
the snow in front of him and up shot a little white cloud
mixed with flakes of snow. What a sight!

Behind Peter men's voices shouted, "Lie down — lie
flat!" and just as he was about to obey, someone else
shouted, "Run! Run!" He could understand that, and he
could run.

But where? Straight ahead. Right away from the
meadow, that was clear, because on both sides the men
were shouting and waving. He ran on quick feet wearing

new shoes. Now that the shooting had stopped he could hear how the bear under his arm growled at each step. From behind a wall of snow which appeared in front of him, he heard the strange voices more clearly. For a moment he wondered how he was to get over the wall, and then a big hand gripped him and pulled him to the other side. He landed on his back among a crowd of boots, legs, rifles and men's faces, which laughingly greeted him.

"Ha, ha, comrade boy! Flag of truce, soldier, little red friend!"

A voice ordered them to be quiet and a man pulled him to his feet and pushed his head behind the snow barrier.

"Sit down!"

Obediently Peter sat down in the snow. The soldiers laughed and joked a little over their small prisoner; one of them took Peter's red cap and waved it above the rampart; and this piece of audacity earned him a shot from across the meadow, which zinged into the snow.

But this one shot ended the lull. For a short while the war had held its breath over a small boy, but now he was forgotten and the battle started again. Bullets tore back and forth. The soldiers lay behind the barricades; they had picked up their weapons and now they fired, reloaded and fired again.

The man who had pulled Peter over gave quick orders and went to and fro so that Peter had time to look at him. Above his heavy top-boots he wore muddy-brown trousers, a loose fur coat fell from his shoulders and on his chest there glistened a couple of stars. The man did not wear a fur hat like the others, but a broad army cap. His face was as yellow as Herr Hantusch's, but smoother and younger. Above his high cheekbones, his slanted eyes occasionally looked down at the child, and when he passed by, his mouth, covered by a dark moustache, spoke strange, soft words. Then he forgot the boy and shouted again at his men.

For a while longer shots still came from the outskirts of the town. Then the noise stopped, began once again, and at last stopped forever.

It seemed to Peter that it was even quieter than it had been this morning in the street, when all the people were running away. The town lay so quiet and still, as if it were afraid. His mother was in the town and also Herr Hantusch, who could not run with his lame leg anywhere near as quickly as Peter could, and all the men who had hidden in the hedge, and the cat — and the thrush. There always was a lot of life in the town. But now they were all afraid. Peter could feel it, and for the first time his heart began to quake.

Perhaps it was only because he was cold. He still sat in the snow as the man had ordered him to do. His cap had lain where it had fallen, his ears were cold; but just at this moment someone leaned over him and pushed it on his head, not gently and lovingly as his mother did but carefully and exactly as perhaps Father would have done.

But it wasn't Father. It was the yellow man who had returned, with a happy smile on his face; he stood in front of Peter like a giant, buttoning up his coat.

"Great victory," he laughed. "Good town if all the children are like you." At least he spoke like other men even if he sounded rough and harsh.

"Stand up!"

And Peter stood up. He reached as far as the man's hip and had to bend his head over backwards in order to look him in the face. He stared at him with big serious eyes and just as seriously the man gazed back at his prisoner.

"Name."

Peter breathed his little verse: "Peter Reisiger, five years old, Ten Middle Road."

"Oho," laughed the man. "Very young soldier! Very young comrade." Then he became serious again. He had laughed, and at the same time his eyes had looked so sad and dark that Peter couldn't understand why, and, just as quickly, light and shade passed over Peter's face.

"Not cry, Pietr Petrovich, comrade boy, not cry! Ten Middle Road? We look for Mother, you and I!"

"Mother is waiting outside the door," said Peter and he wanted to go quickly, but the man seized his hand and held it firmly.

"No, no, not by the door, not waiting! You and I we wait one day, two days, then we look for Mother."

At this moment he looked toward the town and Peter followed his gaze. Far away there was shooting between the houses; the town, which had lain quietly under the morning sky, suddenly became as noisy as a fair, and an airplane high in the sky came screaming down. As it tore up again into the sky, the shrill shouting in the town merged together with the blast of the bombs.

"The bridge," said the man, grinned broadly, and made a gesture as if something fell apart.

"Smashed?" asked Peter, horrified. "Ships go under it and the train goes over it into the wide world!"

"No ship, no train, no world. Bridge broken, ship broken, world broken." Once again that sounded so sad that Peter pressed himself close in order to console the man who had helped him. But in his heart he was afraid; if everything had to be smashed because of a war, then war was a sad and terrible thing.

The man knelt down beside the child, picking up Peter's bear which some soldier had stamped into the snow as the storm broke over the town. The bear now had a crooked face but he still growled. The man waved him thoughtfully to and fro.

"I have got a Peter too," he said in a friendly way. "He's called Nikolai. And a girl called Katja. Dear little bear for Nikolai and Katja. Nice little brother."

Peter reached quickly for the bear and the man gave it to him. He said slowly and clearly: "Listen, Peter, listen; now understand, Peter. You're a child, I'm Father. Soldiers are bad, Father cares for child. Tomorrow we'll look for Mother. Today Peter comes with Father."

He bent down once more and gently patted him on his red cap. His hands were big, hard and yellow, but they were quite friendly and Peter wasn't afraid of them. He put his little hand into the large strong one which held his firmly, and they climbed out of the snow trench. They passed a man who was asleep bent over the parapet; his cap had fallen from his head but he had a young, happy, peaceful face.

"Dead man also father," said the yellow man. "Had nice children at home."

He sounded sorry, but Peter did not know why, because the sun was shining so clearly, and the snow was soft. The man and the child made a wide detour around the fallen men and followed the tracks which tanks had made in the snow covering the plowed land.

They reached a barn and stopped in front of the doorway. Once more the man bent over the child and spoke to him warningly.

"Inside many soldiers, good and bad men, good and bad comrades. Say quickly, try it out: Father, Little Father."

"Father, Little Father," said Peter and was surprised how easy it sounded, although his real father was dressed from his boots to his cap in quite different clothes and had a much different face.

3

Where Is Mother?

Hᴵꜱ new father pulled open the barn door and a
loud uproar greeted them: laughter, calls, shouts,
screams, banging of hammers, shaking of chains and ma-
chinery; and in between a soft, unbroken moaning and
sighing. You could cut the air with a knife; it was thick
and smelled horribly of many smells which Peter
couldn't distinguish.

Neither the noise nor the smells appeared to disturb
Peter's new father. He took Peter with him further into
the barn. There burned a fire which was surrounded by
brown faces, and above it a long pole turned around and
around, from which a pig hung. It was baked brown, and
its legs stuck straight out in front of it. From its crack-
ling, the fat dropped into the fire and sizzled and splut-
tered.

The men jumped up as Father came in; one said something in crisp guttural language. Father waved, and
together with the flame of the fire the noise rose up once
more.

Father placed the boy in front of him, looked down at

him and then looked each man straight in the face and
spoke: what he said sounded serious and severe, as if it
were an order.

The men looked at Peter thoughtfully and quietly; one
or two of them laughed and muttered; another put his
hand up to his cap: "Little general, little comrade, little
boy." Then the pig became more important to them, and
they took knives out of the tops of their boots and cut
large slices of meat out of the back. It had a delicious
smell, and Peter discovered that he was really hungry.

Father thought of that too. He took Peter straight
through the barn, and everywhere the soldiers moved
back. In one corner the wounded were lying; a man bent
over them and bound white bandages around their arms
and legs. Father tapped him on the back, and the man
stood up, turned around and was — a woman, in trousers. She was thick and fat and had a friendly face; her
eyes were as slanted as Father's eyes, and as she looked at
the child they became warm and soft. "A child — here in
the middle of the soldiers!"

"Ljuba!" the soldiers called her, "Ljuba!" They called
until Ljuba bent over them, and then at last they were
quiet. Peter could understand very well that when the
wounded soldiers called Ljuba they really meant their
mother.

Father was now sitting at a table; a group of men
waited for his orders, and as he gave them, one after the
other disappeared. Suddenly the barn door sprang open

and a group of shouting soldiers rushed inside. They had pushed their caps to the backs of their heads and their faces were red and angry.

Father jumped up and shouted and the group scattered, and then Peter, looking outside, saw that, with the butts of their rifles, they were pushing men and women from the town in front of them. What were they doing here? Surely it was nice enough for them at home. Peter looked on curiously — he was very interested. Mother had often said that he wanted to see everything, to know everything — to discover the world.

He discovered Herr Hantusch immediately, looking more bent and yellow than ever. His watery blue eyes looked around and when they suddenly alighted on Peter they opened wide with astonishment.

"Peter, Peter!" screamed Herr Hantusch, with horror, as though this were a dreadfully dangerous place for a small child. Of course he didn't know anything about Peter's new father. Herr Hantusch wanted to say something more, but a soldier pushed his rifle into his back and the old man was quiet.

But the one word that Herr Hantusch might have said was "Mother," and that would have done Peter's heart good, because Herr Hantusch knew something about her — was she here too?

Peter looked at the cold, bedraggled crowd but he didn't find his mother. She hadn't come with them. She must still be at home standing in front of the door and

waiting. He had better be quick! He wanted to tell his
new father, if only he'd come! Peter stood on his tired
feet in the barn doorway and recognized one acquaint-
ance after another among the people from the town.

Near Herr Hantusch was his youngest daughter Clare.
Last Christmas she had tobogganed with Peter down the
hillside and her long pigtails had hit him in the face.
Now she was holding on to Herr Hantusch's arm with
both hands and shivering — it was extremely cold. One
of the soldiers stood in the barn doorway, arms akimbo,
and looked at her from her head to her feet. Clare
pressed more tightly against her father and they both
looked the soldier in the face and waited.

Suddenly Peter cried: "Clare — Clare!" It was horrible here when they were all so frightened, and he
wanted to go away. "Mother, Mother!"

As if he were one of her wounded, Ljuba pressed her
great white hand over his mouth, turned him around,
took him back into the barn, and talked quietly to him.

"Come, little boy. Come, my little son! War is bad for
children, bad for everybody."

Out of her trouser pocket she pulled a piece of sugar
candy and pushed it into Peter's mouth. "Sugar," she
said. "Good, good."

The sugar was certainly good and Ljuba too. She took
him to a heap of straw over which a cloth had been laid,
undid his rucksack, unbuttoned the red jacket, took off
his shoes and rubbed his cold feet — she did everything,

just as Mother used to do. As she took his cap off his head she stood still for a second and looked in fascination at his fair hair, bent quickly and kissed him on the forehead. She smelled just as men smell, but still, she was a mother.

She went away and came back with a plate which smelled of fish and cabbage. She sat down beside him and fed him one spoonful after another, and Peter let her do it although he could have eaten quite well alone. "For Mother," said Ljuba, and while he obediently swallowed the strange food his mother's kind face merged with that of this good ugly woman. "For Father," and Peter didn't know if she meant the Father who was in the silver frame on the writing table, or the new one who was looking after him. The last spoonful, which he should have eaten for Ljuba, had to be put back on to the plate because Peter had suddenly fallen asleep.

Next morning Peter awoke and saw Clare looking down at him, smiling at him out of her sad eyes.

"Peter, Peter," said Clare, quite happy now although she had been crying. Peter beamed with happiness.

"Where is Mother?"

"Thank God, not here — thank God, she probably got away," Clare said, and knelt down beside him. "Ljuba is good, Ljuba fetched me because she saw that you knew me."

Just at this moment Ljuba called her and she sprang

up and went to help her bandage the wounded soldiers who were continually being brought in. Peter looked toward the two women as they went to and fro. Ljuba stroked the wounded on their foreheads just as she had done to him, and they became quiet. Wherever Ljuba and Clare were, there wasn't any more war.

Clare came back and bent over him, saying quickly, "When your new father comes you must tell him that my father is here."

"Aren't you glad that Herr Hantusch is here too?"

"Ah, Peter! Your new father must help him. Say: 'Herr Hantusch is my friend; Herr Hantusch is old and ill, Herr Hantusch must go home.' Your father must let him go — he can do anything."

"Yes, he can," Peter said proudly.

Father was already here and Clare ran off. Father stood over him, enormous and friendly, with shiny, polished boots.

"Slept well, little boy?"

Peter held out his hand to him, and Father took it.

"Herr Hantusch is here, Father."

"Really, and where is Herr Hantusch?"

"With all the others; they're cold and they're crying."

"Oh yes," said Father, "that's war."

"But Herr Hantusch is old and sick — he's supposed to look after me; he promised Father. He's my friend."

Father frowned and bit his lips. "What am I supposed to do about it?"

"You've got to let him go."

Father's face took on a strange, stiff and severe expression. It wasn't Father's face anymore. It was that of a strange soldier, even perhaps an enemy.

"I can't do that."

Peter wanted to turn around and go away. Clare was bending over a wounded man and behaved as if she hadn't heard anything, but her shoulders were shaking and he knew she was crying.

"Father," cried Peter. "Little Father."

"Get up. Come with me and show me Herr Hantusch."

Peter jumped up, shook off the blanket, and Ljuba came quickly and pulled on his shoes; the untied laces dragged behind him as they went outside.

How lovely the fresh air smelled; the sky was the blue of silk, the sun shone and it was cold; somewhere a bird was whistling.

They came to a lattice gate and from here they could see the whole farmyard; it wasn't very big and it was surrounded by a strong, high fence. In one of the corners there was a sheep pen. In the summer Herr Laugemann's sheep had lived there and Mother had shown them to Peter. Now just as many people were gathered inside and they were guarded by soldiers.

"Herr Laugemann's sheep live here," Peter said. "It's not a place for people!"

Father paused and looked darkly at the crowd of people who had gathered in a frightened way around the hut. They were all waiting, frozen and hungry. Suddenly Peter shouted, "There's Herr Hantusch. He's sitting on the steps of the shepherd's hut and he's blowing into his hands. He hasn't seen us!"

"Call him!" Father said.

"Herr Hantusch — Herr Hantusch!" Peter's voice called shrilly.

Herr Hantusch stood up slowly.

"Come here!" Father ordered, and his voice sounded sharp and angry.

Herr Hantusch obeyed. It seemed almost as if he would rather have remained where he was.

"Quick, quick!"

At long last he stood in front of them. Peter wanted to say: "Good morning, Herr Hantusch," but his new Father pulled him back. Herr Hantusch shook all over — it might have been the cold — for his watery eyes looked firmly into Father's face. The guards grinned.

"Let him go!" Father said to the guards, but the old man did not seem to understand that he could go home. Suddenly Father was angry and stamped in the snow: "Quick! March! Get out!" Herr Hantusch bent as much as his stiff back would let him and took Peter's face between his shaking hands.

"Peter, Peter!"

Peter looked fearfully at Father, but his anger had

passed, and Herr Hantusch said quickly: "Be good to him; his mother . . ."

He didn't get any further. A guard struck him in the back with his rifle and Father didn't stop him. Herr Hantusch ran whether he wanted to or not, half falling among the apple trees; he climbed over the wall of snow and ran across the meadow toward the town.

The soldiers laughed, Father slapped his thigh and laughed and in the end Peter laughed too. Then one of the soldiers lifted his rifle up to his shoulder and sent a couple of shots after Herr Hantusch. Certainly they were not meant to hurt him, and they fell into the snow, for Herr Hantusch had already reached the hedge and had disappeared down the garden path. He'd soon find his cat and — Mother.

4

The Journey Begins

"WHAT are you crying for?" and then Peter realized that he wasn't laughing but was crying. Father crouched in the snow and carefully unbuttoned his uniform; he pulled out a leather case, turned it over and handed Peter a picture.

"Nikolai and Katja," he said softly. "Little brother, little sister, and Mother."

So that was the other Mother. She looked like Ljuba but much younger and much prettier. And Nikolai was a nice boy and Katja a nice girl, with her brown eyes and her smooth black hair. But unfortunately the children weren't here; here there were only Ljuba and Clare and the soldiers who shot when Herr Hantusch went home. And Peter began to cry again and cried so long that Ljuba took him and pushed sugar into his mouth. But the sugar wasn't sweet enough to stop his sorrow.

The next day Peter awoke to an unusual stillness. He looked around with a beating heart. The barn was empty, all the wounded had gone and the soldiers must have moved out during the night. Father was nowhere to be seen. Had they all forgotten about him? He pulled off the blanket and ran to the barn doorway; there was Ljuba standing staring at the rising sun. He could see that she had been crying.

"Do you cry often, Ljuba?"

But Ljuba didn't answer. She pulled him through the empty barn, past the carved-up pig and the empty petrol cans to the straw mattress where his shoes were. She tied the laces, grumbling at him. Peter wasn't listening.

"Where are the soldiers?"

"Gone away," Ljuba said shortly.

"Well, and where are Clare and all the people from town?"

"Gone away," Ljuba said again.

"Were they allowed to go home like Herr Hantusch?"

"*Njet, Njet,*" Ljuba answered loudly, "not home; snow, ice, a long, long road."

"When are they coming back again?"

"I don't know." She pulled Peter to her and cradled him in her arms. "Poor women, poor children, poor old people." So *that* was what she was crying about.

Before Peter could ask any more questions Father appeared. He came across the meadow, stopped by the apple trees and waved to Peter that he should come. Peter was already running and his new father opened his arms wide and caught him.

"We're going to look for Mother," Father said. Although this was cheerful news it sounded sad, and Father's eyes looked thoughtfully toward the town which lay as still and quiet as on that morning when Peter's journey had begun — no, it was even quieter. There was no smoke from the chimneys — no sounds, no voices in the streets. As if he were bewitched Peter took Father's hand and went into the town. Where was Mother?

Middle Road was quite empty. But how queer it looked! The snow which had fallen during the night had not been sufficient to cover up everything which lay around. Someone must have had a lot of fun in throwing as much as possible out of the windows onto the street. They had begun with the windows, and they lay all over the place, with their bent frames and broken glass. And then chairs and tables had been thrown after them. There were small cupboards, beds, pillows split open and now filled with snow — pictures, vases, plates and books.

"Here's our house!" Peter cried and tried to pull away from Father's hand, but Father held him firmly. "Mother, Mother!" he called. "I'm here!" But Mother wasn't there.

The front door hung crookedly in its framework; the stairs were broken and above them the doors stood wide open.

"Mother!" But now he was suddenly afraid. His heart beat and his throat was quite tight. The little hallway where Mother always stood when he came home was

empty, and from the wide open bedroom doors only
coldness and confusion met him.

Father said quietly: "She's not here."

No, no, it was no good her being here as it looked now!
As long as Peter could hold on to Father's hand he was
quite good and quiet. He wasn't surprised anymore. It
was like that too in the fairy tales that Mother told: little
boys slept at night and then everything was changed. A
hut became a palace — or the other way around; a king
turned into a beggar — or the other way around; a cat
became a person, a person a bear, and at the end the
mothers always appeared again.

The wardrobe door lay splintered in the middle of the
bedroom, and beside it lay Mother's lovely blue dress,
dirty and torn.

"That's Mother's dress," Peter said, and bent over it
and stroked it.

Father didn't answer; he just stood stiffly in the middle
of the mess. Peter ran here and there, looked and found,
and searched again: his half-burned rocking horse looked
at him out of its glass eyes; his red slippers were lying
near the stove; his train no longer had a chimney, but
still, the wheels went around and that was enough. He
crouched near Mother's silk dress, pushed it to one side
and drove the engine and the broken freight car.

Father loomed over him, looking down at the child.
He held a picture in one hand which he carefully took
out of its broken frame. The happy, open face of a Ger-

man soldier looked back at him; without question it was Peter's own father — the same happy eyes, and the curl over his forehead.

Father went to the window where the curtains were hanging out above the street. Behind the child was playing, and in front of him lay the ruined town. Somewhere in the east the unknown father had disappeared, and somewhere the mother was wandering, searching for her child.

Peter's new father took the picture of his own family out of his pocket and looked at it for a long time. They seemed to be speaking to him.

Nikolai said: "What sort of a boy is he?"

Katja said: "Bring him here."

Mother said: "A little boy can do nothing about this."

The strange father said: "I'll trust you with him."

The door creaked behind them and Herr Hantusch's cat glided into the room. She recognized Peter, jumped up to him, rubbed against his leg and wove her tail around his arm. And then Peter awoke from his dream; his train was broken, and the rocking horse had been burned, and here was this awful mess, and Mother wasn't here anymore. He was alone with a strange soldier in a horrible world and he screamed.

"Peter, little Peter, little boy!" With one leap the strange soldier was beside him and put his arm about him.

"Don't cry, don't worry. Father will take you to Nikolai and Katja; Father will bring you home to Mother."

"To Mother!" Peter swallowed hard and then Father dried his eyes and wiped his nose for him. Then, even if they were both thinking of different mothers, there was still some love somewhere in the world.

Father had said that they'd soon go on a journey.

"We're leaving," Peter said and was happy. Together they walked back through the deserted streets to the barn.

Ljuba packed Peter's rucksack, while Father stood astride his soldier's kit-bag putting in the things Ljuba passed to him. Perhaps she was going with them. But Peter wasn't able to think any further about what would become of Ljuba. He was looking at something else. Ljuba had it in her hand and held it out to Father, who took it quickly and pushed it into his kit-bag: it was blue, with colored flowers. Peter screamed, "That's Mother's silk dress!" and his heart jumped, either from fear or joy; he pulled it to him and pushed his face into the soft silk and smelled his mother's perfume — it really was as if his mother were near.

Father bent his head, and his face was tinged a light red. His eyes were dark and lost: "For Mother," he said hesitatingly.

"Are we going to meet her then? Shall we find her?" asked Peter.

Peter let go of the dress and Father pushed it quickly into the bag; he didn't answer and then Peter understood that they were both thinking of different mothers.

Father was cross with him and a strange light glittered in his eyes. What had Peter done?

Ljuba took his hand and led him rapidly out of the barn.

Together they went to the station, Father in front, Ljuba and Peter behind. Peter had his rucksack on his back with the bear looking out of the top.

"I'm glad, Ljuba, I'm terribly glad that you're coming too!"

"*Njet, njet*," said Ljuba. "Father goes home, Ljuba goes with soldiers."

"Where to, Ljuba?"

"Don't know. Get on a train, get off a train; that's how it is with soldiers."

They arrived at the station where two trains were standing beside the platform. The rusty engines had gotten up steam, but they would not go for some time. Father took hold of Peter and put him beside the luggage. He said angrily, as if he were still cross with him: "Don't do as you did with your Mother! Don't run away!"

No, never again! Where could he go? Besides, there was so much to see that he was quite willing to sit quietly. More and more soldiers ran with their luggage up and down the train, jumped inside and jumped out again, made a detour around Peter, hit him playfully with their bundles, laughed and pretended to seize his bear, shouting, "Home, home to Russia!"

Toward the end of the platform were freight cars which drew up slowly and were attached to the train which was going to Russia. Not all the cars were covered. Guards stood beside some of them with rifles in their hands, and behind them were crowded sick, dirty prisoners.

"Bread — water!"

In Peter's imagination the picture of his mother was merged with that of his almost forgotten father, who had worn the same sort of gray uniform as these men when Peter had seen him last. When was that? A long, long time ago. And now his father was a prisoner, and he was hungry and thirsty.

Peter was already running; he heard his own father call. In his trouser pocket Peter had the piece of bread which Ljuba had given him this morning. He wanted to take it to his father. Peter stood beside the freight car in front of the gray, puzzled and tired faces and couldn't see his father.

"Is Father here?"

A hand suddenly shot out and took the bread from him, and a hungry mouth swallowed it. Then the guards pushed the prisoners back and Peter doubled up to avoid a boot which came behind him. A strong hand pulled him back.

"Peter!" And once again, as he had already done many

times, his new father shouted at the soldiers that this was
his son and heaven help those who harmed him! Obediently the soldiers listened, grinned broadly and were suddenly friendly. But Father was angry with Peter.

"I said never again, do you hear? The prison cars with
German soldiers are forbidden!"

But in spite of all his crossness and his swearing, Peter
felt that he was so cross only because he was fond of him.
"Come, get on with it, get in!" said Father, and was once
more friendly.

He stopped in front of a carriage, helped Ljuba lift his
kit-bag in, jumped up and pulled Peter inside. As he
was halfway up in the air Peter looked around: "Ljuba,
Ljuba!" The train whistled, and puffed white clouds over
the platform which completely hid Ljuba. Then it began
to move and when the cloud had disappeared they were
already out of the station. Ljuba stood small and lonely
on the empty platform and waved, and Peter lifted his
red cap from his head and waved back.

5

The Long Line to the East

THE train rattled on the whole day without halting. It was stuffy in the carriage because the windows were closed, and the stove in the center smoked when they stoked it with wood. Peter was surprised how big such a carriage looked from the inside; in spite of the wooden benches at the sides, and in spite of the luggage which the soldiers had brought with them, he could walk about as if he were in a room.

But he always seemed to be in the way. The soldiers, who were occupied in making themselves comfortable, pushed him here and there; they did it laughingly because they were going home, where their own children were waiting for them, and this was the son of their officer. At last Father rescued him, and put him on the topmost of the two benches which he had reserved for Peter and himself, and showed him the little window so that Peter could look out.

But the town for which he was looking had already disappeared. A long way behind, where the sky met the earth, there was a crooked church tower. Once in the distance he saw the glittering ribbon of a river and, as the train came nearer, the ice blocks which were swirling around on the water, and a gray barge which puffed out smoke through its chimney. There was nothing to be seen of the white boats which had been on the river in summer when Peter had stood with his mother on the bridge, and of the bridge, nothing but twisted, broken rails. It stopped completely where it should have crossed the river.

"Father, the bridge!" Peter called to his father who sat on the bench below him.

"Smashed," Father said easily.

"Who did it?"

"War!" Father answered just as shortly.

"But people have to cross it — Herr Hantusch and Clare —"

"Well, they can't," Father said. "Come down and play with your bear."

But the bear had a silly crooked face and knew nothing about war and bridges.

"When I am big I shall build bridges," said Peter taking a deep breath, "and fix all the broken ones."

"Of course," Father said.

Suddenly Peter thought of something.

"Is my train in your rucksack? You can give it to Nikolai, because he's quite little. He's never traveled as far as I have."

Father looked at the child and laughed a little.

"That's why I packed it," he said.

"And Mother gets the silk dress — and Katja? What's Katja going to get?"

They looked at each other, and when Father took the trouble to look friendly and kind they understood each other well.

"The bear," said Peter, "Katja can have him." He pulled the bear out of his rucksack and laid it on Father's knee.

The Russian officer sat there holding the toy that a German child had given him for a little Russian girl. The soldiers, who knew him for a hard and severe officer, began to laugh.

"Come here, little stranger! Come here, little Peter, little German soldier."

And Peter went from hand to hand, was spoiled — and enjoyed himself.

Now began the first of many nights which he was to spend in the train among the soldiers.

"Come, it's time you slept," said Father.

He wasn't a very clever nurse, and Peter missed Ljuba. But even so Father managed to wrap him up in a blanket and to settle him comfortably on the lowest bench.

One of the soldiers, who was called Idris, came over and pulled off Peter's shoes, took his cap off his head and put both of them carefully under Peter's blanket.

"Mother always puts my shoes under my bed!"

The man appeared to understand, because he laughed,
and when he did so his crooked eyes became slits and his
little black pointed beard shook, and his moustache,
which fell in two long strands over his lips, quivered with
pleasure.

"Hold on to them, little stranger! They're good
leather! Hold on to them!"

He could speak only a little broken German, but his
voice was soft and his hands were gentle. He sat near
Peter on the bench and hummed a sad little tune; his
eyes opened and he gazed at the child with a strange, secret look. He seemed to Peter like the man in the moon
that his mother had described, so he must have come
from a long way off.

"Shall Idris sing to you?"

The little boy lay back and listened, heavy with sleep,
while the train rushed on. Now and again he heard Idris's
dark, strange voice; he didn't understand a word, but he
saw everything as Idris sang: an endless plain covered
with great herds of horses, cows, sheep and camels. Idris
guided the sheep with his long crook.

"Do you live there?" asked Peter.

But Idris wasn't thinking about the child; he was singing for himself or for all the people who were homesick.

One or two soldiers had awakened and they leaned on
their elbows listening to him. First one joined in and
then another. Idris undid his coat, took off his uniform,

and pulled his shirt over his head; as he sat there on the
bench singing, he searched for lice in the creases of his
shirt.

Another soldier joined in the singing — a man called
Ivan.

"Where did you get all those watches?" Peter asked
him.

On his thin bare arm there were five watches close together. Ivan looked at them dreamily, stopped singing
and suddenly cried angrily: "Shut up, you little nui-
sance!"

One or two of the soldiers laughed; then they drew a
deep breath and sang on. Ivan's voice was clear and good.

Between two songs Idris said: "Visit me, Peter, when
the war is over."

Ah, yes! He would love to see the wide plain, and the
foals and lambs. What lovely hands Idris's mother must
have when his were so soft and small. And suddenly sleep
came over Peter's eyes as if Idris's hands had brought it.

Every morning when Peter woke up he would ask:
"Shall we soon be there?"

"Not today," Father would answer. "Russia is very
large."

Sometimes a sudden fear went right through Peter:
what would happen if Father's home was also in ruins,
and the town where he lived broken up?

"The war never came here," Father would answer happily, and it was true. For a long time they had seen no more ruins. The factory chimneys which suddenly appeared out of the desert of snow were smoking, and all the houses in the towns were quite whole. Then came endless forests, endless plains — everything was endless — and everything was covered with snow.

Sometimes they stopped for hours in the shade of a little wood or at a small station made up of wooden houses and sheds. Then the soldiers got out and Idris carried Peter to the platform. The fresh cold air made his eyes sting and he felt dizzy, and then he took deep breaths and was happy.

"Come, run, little boy," Idris said, and he ran with him the whole length of the train, stopping to turn just before the last car.

"Come eat, Petrovich."

He was standing between the soldiers in front of the cookhouse car, and got his share of soup, bread and tea. Then Idris lifted him back into the carriage and with swinging legs they sat and ate in the winter sun. Idris smacked his lips and the sound was full of enjoyment; perhaps one had to do that when the food was so good.

"No, no," laughed Father when he heard Peter copying him. "People like Idris do that; that's what the Kirghiz do."

That entire night the train remained at the station. All

the soldiers scrambled out of their beds. In one corner of the coach Ivan was whispering to a friend, and then he approached Peter and said in a soft voice:

"Give me your shoes, little stranger!"

It sounded quite friendly, but it was an order.

"Hurry up!" and he put his hand under Peter's blanket.

"But they're much too small for you," Peter said fearfully.

Ivan became more and more whining: "Ivan's little boy, Ivanovich, has bare feet in the snow. Give them."

He laughed softly and put his hand heavily on Peter's chest. He pulled off the blanket and there were the shoes, which Idris had polished. Ivan seized them and stood with them under the oil lamp, looked at the soles and the linings and the heels. Then he put his head outside and listened, and Peter saw that his face shone like a Christmas star.

It was silly to be afraid of him if he was only thinking of his own son — that was it. Peter said thoughtfully: "I could give you one and then we shall each have one. Do you really want both?"

He stood up and went over to Ivan, and through a hole in his red stocking his toe looked out.

"Because I really have a long way to go. I've got to look for Mother and I can't do that without shoes."

"Ivan!"

Father's voice came clear and sharp. He had come into

the train carriage without either of them having noticed him. Ivan's beaming face froze; as he swung around
it took on the same expression which he always wore. He
bent down and put the shoes carefully in Peter's arms.

"They're good shoes — good leather. Is Ivan Ivanovich
to freeze?"

Father's face was red with anger. He took the shoes
and put them in his kit-bag. "Go to sleep!" he said quietly, and Peter obeyed.

Ivan waited with bent shoulders under the lamp, but
Father took no further notice of him.

Next day Peter sat beside Idris drinking his soup.
Idris's beard shook, his moustaches hung from his lips
and fell into the soup. Peter sat there fascinated; it was
hard work not to stare.

"The prisoners have to get out today."

"Here?" Peter asked, astonished. "But there isn't anything here."

"You just don't see it," Idris said. "Everything's in the
ground; coal, iron — work."

"For the prisoners?"

"Yes, work for the prisoners."

The train whistled and came slowly to a standstill.
The soldiers pulled open the doors and jumped out into
the snow which covered the edge of the railroad tracks.
Peter wanted to follow them, but Father caught hold of
him by the collar and pulled him back on to the seat.

"You stay here! Understand!"

Peter sat fearfully in the empty carriage and listened. At the end of the train there was noise and shouting. Father's voice appeared to give orders, there was a whistle, and then everything was quiet. Then once more the

shouting began. Peter pulled his bear to him; it was the only friend he had in this strange, frightening world.

Father stood wide-legged in the snow, and Peter heard him counting the prisoners:

"One, two, three . . ."

Silently Peter crept out of the carriage but he couldn't
see his own father anywhere. He saw only the bent, tired
backs in soldiers' faded uniforms, the rags which they
bound around their feet, and their bare heads with the
hair blown by the wind. No, his own father wasn't there
— because he had always been happy, and he stood up
straight and walked firmly. These soldiers stumbled
through the snow almost as if they couldn't go another
step further.

Suddenly Peter noticed that his new father was looking at him and his eyes were big and sad. Ah, good. There
was at least one person that belonged to him. Peter
pressed his face into the folds of Father's coat, and held
on to Father's legs. For the first time he wasn't crying
about himself — but about the prisoners.

Father bent down, picked him up and took him back
to the carriage.

"Now be quiet, Peterkin. You and I, we can't do anything. The day after tomorrow we shall reach home and
find Mother."

Once more there was the magic word that made the
world right again.

Father had promised a little too much, because it took
at least two days more of continuous traveling through
the snowy, hilly land and the thick woods. The branches
of the giant firs hung, laden with snow; then suddenly
the wood became lighter. The birch trees were covered

with a glittering frost and they shone in the sunlight like the Snow Queen's palace.

Toward the end they followed a little river which twisted into a plain, with rushes all along the edge of the water. Then the train stopped and Father said:

"Orenburg! We've arrived."

6

The New Family

FATHER was so excited that he looked much like a child in front of a Christmas tree; he pulled his things down from the bench, opened the door of the carriage, jumped outside and disappeared.

Peter stood on the train step and didn't know what to do; he could see nothing except the white steam of the engine which covered everything. Then the steam dispersed, and Peter saw Father with a little girl in one arm while the other was around the shoulders of a tall woman. A boy was standing beside him wearing a blue-gray uniform with polished boots. So he must also be a soldier, although he wasn't much bigger than Peter. Father seemed to have forgotten Peter completely, but the little boy saw Idris. Among all his soldier friends, Idris had traveled with them the longest, and he still had further to go.

"Don't cry, Peterkin," Idris told him. "Don't forget that Father has to tell Mother that Peter is here."

"Oh Idris, Idris, but it isn't Mother!"

Now Peter was really crying and the tears ran down his

cheeks. He had always hoped, deep inside him, that at the end of the long journey he would find his own mother.

Idris sat down on the top step, put his arms around Peter and said quietly in his ear:

"German boy has German mother, Russian officer has Russian wife — she'll be a good Russian mother for German boy."

But Father hadn't forgotten Peter; he was approaching now with the strange woman, and both the children were running a little in front and staring at Peter. The woman had a broad quiet face, and strangely, she had fair hair just like Mother, that fell in waves under her headscarf. She came quietly toward him; the little girl, who was still in front, carefully took his hand and said with a little curtsy:

"I'm Katja. What's your name, boy?"

She spoke in her own language, but he had heard the same question often enough from the soldiers, and he replied in a voice still full of tears:

"Peter Reisiger, five years old, Ten Middle Road."

They all laughed, Father, Mother, Katja and Nikolai, and the latter saluted like a soldier and said:

"Kolja."

"But your name is Nikolai!" Peter said, and wiped away the last tears.

"When we want to be nice to him we call him Kolja," Father explained. "Mother calls me Nikolai and I call her Elizabeth, and Katja is Katerina, but we call her Katja. Here Mother, here's our little brother, Peter."

Mother took Peter in her arms and kissed him on the cheek. To his astonishment she spoke a careful broken German.

"Did you get lost, little boy? Did you fall out of your nest? Never mind!"

The children chatted away like little birds, but suddenly Kolja became serious; he looked at his father questioningly and then looked strangely at Peter and said, "Is he an enemy?"

But Mother answered once again so that Peter could understand her and this gave him confidence: "A small child can't help the war. We shall all love one another."

At this Kolja put Peter's rucksack on his back and Katja seized his hand and wanted to pull him away.

"Stop, stop," Father called. "Don't forget Idris!"

Peter ran back to him and felt a little ashamed. But Idris wasn't cross; he just seemed quite strange and happy. He bowed in front of Father and the little boy, crossed his hands over his heart and murmured: "Your arms shall be sound, and your legs shall be sound!"

He repeated this again in Russian, and then in his own language, and last of all in German so that Peter could understand his farewell blessing: "Strong legs, strong arms."

"That's how they greet each other in his country," Father said. "You must do the same."

And Peter crossed his hands over his heart, bowed and murmured: "Strong arms! Strong legs!"

Then Idris laughed; he had looked after Peter for a long time, but now the steam clouds from the train covered his face.

They went into the town. Near the station there were huge piles of wood; other places were filled with iron rods and low, clay houses lay in between. Some of them had rush roofs and others wooden shingles. There were also factories with smoking chimneys, where the siren whistled for the change of shift, and from the gates the factory workers poured into the town.

"I took time off because you've come," Mother said, "But tomorrow I shall have to go to work again. Why didn't you wire me that you had the child with you? I haven't had time to get anything ready."

"It doesn't matter," Father assured her. "We've come out of the war. And I decided rather suddenly to bring him with me."

More wooden houses were standing along the sides of the streets now. Under the low-lying roofs pretty garlands of evergreens swung in the air.

In front of the doors there were little porches with steps leading to them. In summer one could probably play under the steps, and Peter could build a little house for himself and the bear. Then it suddenly occurred to him that he was going to give away his bear.

"I've brought you something, Katja," he said. But

Katja couldn't understand him, so Mother had to trans-
late.

"You'll soon learn Russian," Mother told him. "Kolja
will help you."

She led him up the steps into a house which was built
entirely of wood, and they entered a room in which a
huge stove had been built and from which lovely warm
air rushed to meet them.

Katja took the fur cap off her black hair, climbed up
onto the top of the stove, swung her legs and asked for
the bear. Kolja took off his soldier's cap and now he
didn't look much older than Peter. He opened Peter's
rucksack and took out the bear.

It belonged to Katja now, and she sat and nursed it in
her arms while both boys climbed up beside her and
chatted together about the bear, each in his own language.

Peter learned his first Russian words; he learned what
nose, eyes, mouth and legs were. They laughed together,
asked questions, and learned.

Peter understood snatches of their conversation; he
slipped down from the stove and stood in front of a picture of an old bearded man with large dark eyes, which
looked at Peter earnestly. He was wearing golden robes; a
golden halo was painted above his head and blended into
the brown and red-gold shimmer of the background.

"Is that God?"

"No, Peter," Mother said, "even in our country no one

has seen God, and so nobody could paint him. This is a saint who lived a long time ago on the earth, just as we are doing now. He was such a holy man that now that he is dead, he stands near God and prays for us."

"I have always prayed to God and have asked him for things — I asked him if I could travel around the world."

"Yes, Peterkin," Mother answered him. "In every country in the world people pray in different ways to God. I suppose you have never seen an icon before."

"An icon?"

"That's what these gilded religious pictures are called; they used to hang in every Russian home, and even today lots of people still have them."

Father stood up, went to his kit-bag and took out Peter's train — the train without a chimney and the freight car without wheels — but that didn't matter to Kolja who was so glad that his shouts of joy drowned the little conversation that Peter was having with Father.

"Give Mother's silk dress to her."

"Later, Peter," Father said, and looked just as thoughtful as when he had first put it in his bag. So Peter forgot his mother's silk dress and played at trains with Kolja.

"Where are we going to?" Kolja shouted. "To Moscow!"

"The bear wants to go home," Katja whispered and tried to put him in the car. But it didn't seem as if he would get home quickly because he was too big to fit in.

In the evening there was a great discussion as to where
the new brother was to sleep.

"We can't put him on top of the stove because he's
still too small and he'll fall down," Mother said.

"Let *me* sleep on the stove," said Kolja delightedly.
"It's lovely and warm up there; it's the warmest place in
the house."

And to Peter's great astonishment they made up a bed
on top of the oven, and, after the family had knelt a little
while in front of the holy picture, Kolja scrambled up.
Peter was allowed to sleep with Katja in the big feather
bed which was soft as a snow mountain.

Katja and Kolja, who was lying on his tummy on top
of the stove, whispered and chatted laughingly together.
Peter couldn't understand a word, but he wished terribly
that he was big enough to sleep on top of a stove like a
real Russian.

Father and Mother came into the room and Father
looked as if he were cross, and instantly they were quiet.

Mother said: "The children are a bit wild because you
were not here and I go out to work. It's probably like that
everywhere, but perhaps it will do them good now
they've got a little brother whom they'll have to teach.
Go to sleep now, my children, Kolja, Katja, Peter!"

So now he belonged to them; he belonged to her and
she was his mother. But as he fell asleep he suddenly had
the feeling, as he had had so often before on this long

journey, that his real mother bent over him, clear, kind, and dressed in the blue silk dress.

"Don't forget me, my little Peter," she said softly. "A child must always return to his mother."

"I shall certainly come back, Mother," Peter said. "I'll look for you and I'll find you, but for now I want to stay here."

"It's terrible," said his Russian mother to his Russian father, "that there's enmity and war between people, so that a small child should lose his own mother and perhaps never find her again."

"Nobody can know," Father answered. "This child has been lucky so far, and he'll stay here with us. Look, I've brought something; it belonged to his mother, but she would never have gotten it back. Are you glad?"

"Yes, I'm very happy about it," Mother answered and sighed as she took the blue dress.

When Peter woke up the next morning Mother had already gone to work. A huge fire burned in the stove and the porridge was cooking. Kolja slid down from the top, pulled the eiderdown off Katja and Peter, laughed and climbed into his school uniform.

"Katja had better hurry up! She's got to go to the kindergarten."

Father was standing before the little mirror in the living room, shaving. He turned around and waved to the children.

"Ha, that's an industrious family! And we are two lazy people, Peter, what are we going to do?"

"Peter is really big enough to go to school too," Kolja suggested, but Father thought that it would be soon enough when he'd gone back to the army. By then Peter would know more Russian.

"Well, I think he's a smart boy," Kolja said generously, and disappeared.

Katja too had a sort of uniform, a black alpaca pinafore with sleeves puffed at the shoulders. She looked quite nice, but strange. Before she went she helped Peter to dress, laughing at him because he was bigger than she, and so silly! Last of all Father knelt down in front of him and tied his shoelaces because even Katja couldn't do that.

"You must have some felt shoes like Kolja and Katja when it begins to thaw, and then you'll have some fun! We'll go and look for them."

As he went through the town with Father, Peter looked around him. The streets were quite different from those at home. In the wide roadway were deep wheel-ruts, and at the edges the snow had been pressed to a high wall covered with dirty mud. In the center of town the streets were narrower, and above their heads hung colored advertisements and flags. In the shops strange-looking people stood behind the counters.

In the shop where Peter was to get his felt shoes, the

shoemaker looked so much like Idris that he could have
been his brother.

"He's a Kirghiz," Father explained, "like Idris. They
live fairly near here in the steppes and they know how to
make things of felt and leather. Their life is spent with
horses and sheep. They and the Bashkirs bring all the
horses into the town."

"Do they fit you?" asked the quiet man, and Peter decided that you couldn't have anything nicer than felt
boots lined with sheepskin.

He paraded around under the rows of boots which
were swinging from the ceiling, and was very happy.

"You can put your others on in the summer," Father
said and pulled some rubles out of his purse and paid.

They went further, and Peter was as warm and happy
as he'd ever been.

The town was really quite full of horses — Peter had
never seen so many together in his life. Some had been
brought to the market and some were harnessed to little
wagons. On every one of them sat strange people from
the steppes with goods which they had brought to sell in
the town: wooden articles and woven rush baskets, clay
pots, harnesses, huge round cheeses, and bulging leather
bags.

"What's inside?"

"Kumiss. Sour mare's milk — but that's not for children."

Peter shivered; no, certainly he would never drink anything like that.

Then they were standing before the huge cathedral.

"Shall we go inside? Do you want to see the icons?"

Father walked quickly through the doorway and Peter followed.

It was dusk in the high-domed building, but the golden light which streamed in to meet him took Peter's breath away. A whole wall of gold! Close together and on top of one another — pictures! Huge eyes, hands upheld in blessing, and halos painted on a brown-red background.

Father knelt down and Peter did the same, but his eyes wandered around while Father was looking thoughtfully at the pictures. An old man came in quietly. He wore a robe right down to his ankles and a cord around his waist; he had a white beard that hung down to his chest. He bowed before the pictures, took out a cross and knelt down. The soles of his boots, which one could now see, were full of holes. But with all that gold about, who could think of worn-out shoes!

Later he spoke to Father.

"It's not often that an officer comes into my church. And the child?"

"He's a German child," Father said. "The war brought him here; bless him, Father Ivanovich."

The old man laid a big thin hand on Peter's head.

Looking at him with large sad eyes, he held his cross over him and said a prayer.

"Now you're really in Russia," whispered Father, and they tiptoed out.

Outside, the other Russia was going past; a column of singing schoolchildren in their blue-gray uniforms and stiff caps. They moved their arms in rhythm, and they were following a flag which the biggest was carrying. There — of course — was Kolja! He didn't look any different from the others. He wasn't the clown who had teased them from the top of the stove anymore; he had a severe, grown-up face.

"Kolja, Kolja!" Peter shouted. But Kolja looked straight in front of him, seeing neither his father nor the new little brother from Germany.

7

Peter Travels
in the Wrong Direction

Spring came, with storms from the Ural mountains, at the foot of which the town lay. The streets were
like lakes, and then muddy rivers, and then they slowly
dried out — and all at once it was warm. At night huge
swarms of migrating birds flew over the town, and from
their calls Father knew what they were and where they
lived.

"Wild geese, herons, cranes, swans and songbirds," he
said. "They nest in the Kirghiz steppes, in the rushy forests of the steppe rivers, in the salty lakes, or in the light
Ural forests. If only I could take you there!"

But Father had no time to show Peter his native land.
Tomorrow he had to go. Mother cried and Katja lay sob-
bing under the eiderdown, and in her sorrow, became
quite disagreeable. She pushed Peter away when he
wanted to comfort her: "You! You don't know what it's
like, you're not his child!"

"Of course he's our child," Father and Mother said, almost together. And Father patted him on the head and said goodbye. Homesickness for those two other people who were his own parents, and the parting from this kind new Father merged together, and Peter nearly cried too, but he saw an inquisitive look on Kolja's schoolboy face. Tomorrow he would go with him to school, and as Kolja didn't cry Peter also kept his tears back.

It was not until the light had been put out and Kolja and Katja were already asleep that he suddenly felt homesick again. He was now only a very small boy who lay in a strange bed and cried.

He liked it at school. The teacher was a friendly man who wore the same blue-gray uniform as the boys. He allowed Peter to sit beside Kolja as long as he was there as a visitor.

Learning was like a lovely game, and it was just what his alert mind needed. Even if school discipline was as strict as if they were all soldiers, it was still amusing to do the same as the others when the teacher gave an order: to lift his hands up and make believe the clouds were overhead; to clap his hands together and make believe it was thunder, and to take cover from the downpouring rain when the thunderstorm broke. Like all the others Peter learned, with stiff fingers, to write the first Russian letters, and he had no idea that at home the letters were different.

Kolja and Ivan, Boris, Nikita and Wassili were his friends. He learned with them and he played the same games with them that children all over the world play when they are happy together. He had almost forgotten that he wasn't a Russian child, that far away in Germany his own mother missed him and would say to her friends: "I had a little boy who was called Peter; he was five years old when I lost him and he would have been six in the spring."

As far as Peter was concerned it could always be just as it was now. But it wasn't. The heat of the steppes descended on the town, and his new mother said: "When it's a bit cooler, in the autumn, then we shall have the great Feast of the Horses outside the town. The whole town makes a festival of it. From everywhere around riders come with their best horses. The Bashkirs have bred fine animals in the green Ural valleys; the Cossacks come with their general — and they're the best riders in the world."

Peter's heart jumped with joy; he was growing fast and as he saw nothing but horses every day he couldn't think of anything better than to be able to ride. Kolja and he were of the same mind.

Mother said, "We'll put on our best clothes because it's the happiest festival we have, and I'll mend the blue silk dress which Father brought back with him."

Suddenly Peter's joy was gone, and his face became white and stiff. Of course he knew that Mother was kind and he liked her. But he suddenly realized that he no longer knew what his own mother really looked like and it was only the blue dress that reminded him of her. It belonged to her, and no one else ought to have it.

Since Father had gone Peter slept with Kolja, and Katja with Mother. When they went to bed that night Peter forgot the horses; he could think only of his lost mother.

After a while Kolja said suddenly:

"What are you crying for, Peter?"

"I want to go home; I want to find Mother."

Peter threw himself back and shut his eyes. In his mind one thought became more and more clear. Mother had gone and it was dark again. He sat up in bed and shook Kolja awake and said: "You'll have to help me, and you mustn't tell. I'm going home."

"What are you going to do?" Kolja asked, astonished and now wide awake.

"The same way I came here; you get into a train and it goes."

"Yes, that's true," Kolja replied, although he had never been out of his own town.

"There are plenty of trains standing in the station. Now, when there are so many strangers about, it would be quite easy."

"When do you want to go?"

"Tomorrow," Peter answered decidedly.

"But the horses, the big horse fair! Don't you want to wait a little?"

"Not a single day! Horses! I'm going to look for Mother; that's what I want to do, and that's what I'm going to do!"

"But Mother and Katja!" Kolja tried once more. "And Father, what will he say when he returns? You're his son now!"

Then Peter said the same words Katja had said when Father was leaving.

"You don't know what it's like. And if you're not going to help me, I shall go alone."

Once more a sob stuck in his throat, and then he swallowed it and he and Kolja sat in bed and made plans. They crept around the room; through the doorway a small ray of light shone as Mother sat and sewed.

On her way to bed, she was surprised that Peter's rucksack lay on the chair, the red cap on top of it, and that the children were asleep in a half-sitting position with their heads together, as if they were sharing a secret. Mother laughed and put them straight — and left Peter's things where they were.

"Thank you very much; you were all very nice to me," Peter murmured, half-asleep, and Mother laughed once more before she herself fell asleep. She was too tired to suspect anything.

It really was quite easy. Mother and Katja had already

left when the boys got up, both excited conspirators. They hid the rucksack behind some bushes and Peter went to school for the last time, and in the singing lesson learned the song "Russia Is the Most Beautiful Land," and he decided that it might be true if he had been Kolja — but he wasn't really at home here. He was shivering with excitement. In the afternoon they took the rucksack out of its hiding place and crept away to the station. The streets were full of people and no one took notice of the children.

Kolja, who knew every corner, led Peter between the houses and the warehouses to the station.

"Goodness, Peter, you're lucky. There's a freight car, and it's already getting up steam; quick, get in."

Before they realized it, they had to part. Peter had already slipped into the car. He looked carefully out of the doorway but no one had seen them. Outside, Kolja stood at attention like a soldier.

"Give my love to Mother and Katja," Peter said, with a beating heart.

Kolja said earnestly: "I've put your bear in your bag because Katja didn't need him; she only plays with the wooden horse with the colored flowers on its back."

He turned around and slipped away out of the station. Something like loneliness and fear came over the small boy who stood alone in the big train.

He squatted down on the heap of sacks, listened intently to what was happening outside. He hardly dared to breathe when suddenly he heard steps coming near. A man closed the doors. In the half-darkness Peter felt for his bear, found him and hugged him closely. Then a whistle blew, the engine chugged and whistled and the train moved off. They were on their way.

To Mother — to Mother — the train seemed to say.

8

Found by the Kirghiz

THE old Kirghiz, Ibrahim, sat in front of his tent
and stared through his squinting eyes into the sun, which
had just begun to turn the western sky red. The tall
grasses which the heat of a summer in the steppes had
burned yellow were turning to gold. The salt lake which
normally lay dead and quiet under the heavens began to
glimmer.

Ibrahim thought about his son Idris, who had returned
on leave from the army the previous winter. He seemed
to be doing well; he was wearing leather shoes and his
uniform looked just as smart on him as the caftan, with
its red leather belt, the lamb's-wool cap with the green
lining of goat leather, and the long felt boots with their
colored strings. During those few weeks when Idris was
home, he had once more worn his Kirghiz clothes; he was
once again a shepherd, a rider, a hunter and master of all
the cattle.

When the cattle had been tended in the evening, Ibrahim and Idris had sat on the big carpet in the tent, staring at the hole in the roof where the stars shone through,

and told each other tales of the world where there were no steppes. Behind the curtains Idris's young wife, Fatima, put the clay mugs together and brought in wooden dishes with rich-smelling meat for the two men. She gave them jugs of sour mare's milk which they poured into their mugs and drank heartily.

Then it was time for Idris to leave. His father had taken him as far as the station where twice a week a train waited; one went to Russia and the other to China. It was one of the few stops made by trains passing through the central Asian steppes; it was the first stop after leaving Russia.

The stories which Idris had told remained with him. And now, as the sky got redder and redder, Ibrahim thought about the little boy who wore a red cap and had fair hair like straw and eyes like water. He was looking for his mother and had been traveling with a Russian officer toward the east. Idris had been kind to him, just as he was kind to the foals and the lambs. Was it possible that the child had found his mother?

The train going to distant China would come through today. Ibrahim would hear its noise and he would see, far off, the steam clouds when it came into the station. The clear air of the steppes brought the sounds as far as his tent. But today Idris would not come.

Ibrahim waited in the bushes near the salt lake, and the wild geese and the swans came down in the evening light to their nests. Then he heard the whistle of the

train and the clouds of steam slowly covered the sky.
After a while the train went on again; now he had only to
wait for the cattle.

From behind a group of trees a galloping rider with
loose reins appeared. His caftan streamed in the wind
and the piebald horse's hoofs sounded dully on the sandy
ground; a greyhound accompanied him.

The rider swung around and stopped in front of Ibrahim.

"*Chabar bar?*" Ibrahim asked; "Is there any news?"

"*Bar!*" the rider replied; "There is. There's a child
alone in the steppes."

"Did his mother lose him when she was gossiping at
the spring?"

"The child is looking for his mother."

"Why didn't you put him on your horse and bring him
with you? His mother won't find him today."

"I didn't see him," answered the rider. "Volodja, the
Russian who's in charge of the train, found him in a
freight car and pushed him out. The boy must have
slipped aboard the train in Russia."

"But it's nighttime," Ibrahim said, and stood up.

"Wolves only hunt people in the winter," the rider answered. "At this time of year all they take is a lamb here
and there. This is a strange child," he continued, "he's
got hair like straw and eyes like water. He's got on a red
cap, and shoes made of leather. If Allah wishes he'll find
his mother."

"Allah wishes that we shall find *him*," Ibrahim said. "My son, Idris, knew of a child who looked like this one. In the evening a child is hungry, and he's afraid of the night when the owl calls and the bats fly through the moonlight. If Idris were here he would go and look for the child. I'll do so."

"Your horses haven't returned," said the rider.

"My favorite horse is standing behind the tent. Will you wait for me?"

"I'll wait. If the child is not a ghost, then he comes from a long way off. We shall hear news."

Ibrahim returned at once with the black horse, jumped onto its back as lightly as if he were young; he clicked his teeth and they rode away.

It must have been Allah himself, the God of the Mohammedans, who had taken Peter into his care. The reluctant little world-traveler stood alone in the middle of the Kirghiz steppes. He had crept close to one of the big trees and was fearfully watching Ibrahim's four hundred horses and herds of cattle rumbling past; they returned home only at night. They were covered by a cloud of dust and the whole earth shook.

The stallions galloped around with their mares whom they had guarded all day long, accompanied the young animals who were still on their own, and the brood mares who had had foals in the spring. They came past in a wide band, piebalds and Palominos, blacks and browns. In the lead came a gray horse with a boy riding bareback,

cracking a whip. As they reached Peter's tree the herd
divided and passed in two great waves.

Peter pressed his hands to his face and waited for the
flying hoofs to knock him over.

"Tschu!" A voice suddenly thundered near him, and
like a miracle the herd of horses turned away. A hand
seized him by the collar and before he realized it he was
sitting astride the back of a saddled horse. He held on
tightly to the rider, an old man looking like Idris, except
that his beard was white.

"Idris?" He said it aloud and the old man didn't appear astonished.

"My son told me of the strange child," he said in Russian, "now he's come."

"I'm going home," Peter said, still breathless.

"You're traveling east, but your mother lives in the
west. I can see that by your hair and eyes. That train
was going in the wrong direction from your home."

"What shall I do?" Peter asked trustingly.

"You'll stay here with me," Ibrahim said.

Very slowly a second great cloud of dust appeared over
the steppes — the fat-tailed sheep were coming home.
Body to body the flock went past. Two naked boys rode
on one huge ram with their hands pressed into his thick
fleece.

"Tschu!" the old man cried to the ram, and the whole
herd turned short and passed by the tree and the horses.
Then Ibrahim made a sign and they rode toward the

tents. The horses were already standing behind the wicker
fences, while a couple of men were milking the mares.
The sheep pressed on through the open gateway and the
boys sprang off their ram and shut the gate.

They looked curiously at Peter. And now Peter made
the greeting that he had learned from Idris. He crossed
his hands over his heart: "Are your arms and your legs
well?"

"*Amamba*," the boys answered and put their hands on
their chests.

"Are your cattle well?"

"*Amam*."

Suddenly they laughed loudly, took hold of Peter and
pulled him into the tent.

This first evening was the forerunner of many for Peter. They ate their evening meal in the tent; its thick felt
walls were cool in summer and warm in winter, and because Ibrahim was rich they were hung with carpets.
There was also a carpet over the grass under their feet.
Peter was allowed to sit in Idris's place and the boys, who
were his sons, lounged on the low sheepskin couch on
which they also slept. Ibrahim, as master of all the herds,
sat on the raised seat of honor.

The news of the boy from the west traveled quickly
through the steppes and guests arrived almost every day
to see him.

Idris's wife, Fatima, and the other women worked behind the curtained hangings. They came in and brought the men and boys food to eat and drink.

Peter learned very quickly to put his fingers into the big dish and to fish out the meat, and only at the end did he use the wooden spoon to ladle out the spiced sauce. And, like Ibrahim and the boys, he belched when it tasted good; he also smacked his lips as they did. At the end of the meal he was allowed to drink a tumbler of kumiss, mare's milk, which Father Ibrahim poured out of the leather gourd; it tasted sour and sweet. Every evening the tent — with the hole on top through which the stars shone — began to sway gently in the breeze and made Peter dream.

In the mornings before the herds were driven out, Ibrahim spread the prayer carpet in front of the tent, walked into the middle, bowed deeply toward the west and lay with his face on the colored wool and prayed to Allah.

He did this again every evening. After Ibrahim his boys prayed and very soon Peter also belonged to them, so that he too bowed before Allah, the God of the Mohammedans, when the prayer hour came around. Soon he was running around naked like Isak and Mahmed, Idris's sons; he had lost all fear of the animals and he joined in the wonderful games which children of the steppes play.

They taught him how to press his legs into the ram's side and how to guide it by pulling the thick coat. He

rode with them to watch the flocks when they went to
the summer pastures near the river. Behind them the red
dust cloud raised by four thousand hoofs spread into the
sky, and the bleating of the rams and the sheep and the
lambs sounded like many bells.

Isak was the elder and knew more than his brother.

"Do you want to see how we catch wild horses?" he
asked one day. Taking a rope, as the herd of mares passed
by, he threw it around a foal, who reared and tried to get
away. But Isak had already got his legs around its stomach, and in the end it had to give in.

Peter would not be able to learn how to do it this year,
but next year or the year after that — who knows? He
wanted to be like Isak; quick, brave, clever and happy.

They sheared the sheep beside the little spring; they
helped Fatima who was busy ornamenting a red cap for
her small daughter; and Peter helped to choose the colored wools which they used for carpet-making.

Then he talked about his mother. The more he lived
this life the fainter his mother's face became, but Fatima
possessed the same kindness and friendliness which his
almost forgotten mother had.

"I want to find her, but not right away," Peter said,
and Fatima laughed. She had gotten used to the fact that
her third son had fair hair and was the wildest of them
all.

It was now wintertime, the first — or the second since
he had been lost? Peter couldn't count the time any-

more. The children wore warm clothes made of foal
skins; Fatima had made him a caftan lined with sheep's
wool and the belt which held it together was red.

Outside, between Ibrahim's tent and the tents of all
his relations, the cattle were herded behind a fence. They
lay close together in the snow and warmed each other.
During the day they scooped the snow away and ate the
hard steppe grass. They became very thin before the
spring came, but then suddenly the whole steppe
bloomed and they all had enough to eat and grew thick
and fat.

But one night in the middle of the winter, the boys
were awakened by a long, drawn-out howl. The grey-
hounds outside began to bark; the horses grew restless
and the stallions neighed.

Isak said: "Wolves! Even if Mother forbids it, I'm going after them this year!"

Ibrahim had been awakened too.

"Come with me," he said, and Isak jumped up and
went outside with him. Fatima came in trembling and
sat down beside the boys under the fur rug.

"If only Idris were here! He hunts wolves just as he
does horses — he's very strong and brave."

When the hunters started shouting the wolves
stopped howling, and early the next morning the men
returned. As he always did, Ibrahim spread out the prayer
carpet, knelt down and prayed, and then he showed the
boys a dead wolf. As Isak had killed it, he was now re-

garded as a man by the other two boys. He pulled open the wolf's jaws and showed them its huge teeth.

"It was a very old and clever wolf," he said, "but I was even more clever."

9

Smuggled into China

Once more a summer passed and then a winter. Spring came and the migrating birds appeared out of the sky and made their nests in the reeds. Then a rumor traveled with the speed of a rider from tent to tent.

Long before anyone had seen him, they all knew that Fu Tsin, the Chinese, was on the way; he came every two or three years with his caravans to bring silk to Tashkent and Samarkand. He came with his own camels, ignoring the trains, because he loved to travel right through the steppes just as his father and his grandfather had done before him. He traveled on the old "silk" road where once silk from China was brought to the west. Now and then, on his return journey, he went off his route and visited the tents where his old friends lived.

Ibrahim was such a friend. Since he knew that Fu Tsin was on the way he was waiting for him. Fatima prepared the most delicious dishes, and evening after evening she put on her jewels, and the boys wore clothes, although they usually ran around with nothing on.

Then one evening, on the horizon they saw the long necks of the camels approaching with their swinging gait. Some camels were saddled and carried riders, while others were loaded with goods.

One camel knelt down in front of Idris's tent and Ibrahim helped a tall thin man to get down and asked after the state of his arms and legs. The stranger answered in a language Peter couldn't understand, but which sounded very polite.

At the doorway of the tent, which had been pulled open, he was given a bowl of water to wash his hands, and Peter held the towel. With delicate fingers the man concluded this customary gesture while staring at the fair-haired child, of whom he had already heard as he rode through the steppes. But he said nothing. Politeness forbade curiosity.

Ibrahim and Fu Tsin sat in the seats of honor, and the boys squatted on the carpet at their feet and listened.

Fu Tsin spoke first of the political situation in China, then at last he asked about what he really wanted to know.

"Where did you find him, what's his name, and how old is he? Are you going to keep him, my good Ibrahim?"

"He's my grandsons' youngest brother. Nobody even thinks about his not being a Kirghiz. Stand up and tell our guest your name!" And Peter said his little verse.

"Peter Reisiger, five years old, Ten Middle Road."

Nobody understood him, and neither he nor they realized how the years had passed and that his age was wrong. Fu Tsin bent his head.

"If he were a Chinese, he would have to return to his father's house, to pray to the spirits of his ancestors."

"How can he go home?" Ibrahim answered. "He lives a long way to the west. A Russian brought him to the East because the war has robbed him of his father and mother."

"Even so, he must go home," the Chinese insisted.

"He's quite happy here," Ibrahim said sadly. "I would never put him on a train going to the west. How could he find his way home over the mountains and rivers, across Russia. I couldn't let him go alone — he's still a little boy."

Behind the curtains Fatima was crying quietly.

"Give him to me to take to China," Fu Tsin said. "You are quite right, Ibrahim, he certainly can't go to the west. But the great river flows through my country to the sea, and there are ships which could take him home. Perhaps one of my friends would take him to the south over the Heavenly Mountains. Either he'll go on a junk to the sea, or on a camel's back to India. Give him to me, so that this may come to pass."

"Take him with you then," Ibrahim said. Tears came into his eyes and the Chinese stared at him, astonished. He was not used to people showing their feelings.

"Do you love him, Kind Grandfather?" he asked softly.

"Yes, I love him," Ibrahim answered sadly, and pulled at his rat-tail moustache. "Go to bed, my grandsons! Our honored guest must also sleep."

As they fell asleep Isak asked: "Are you happy?"

"Of course, Mother —"

Somewhere his real mother was saying: "If he's still alive he'll be eight years old this spring. But he won't remember me."

"— Fu Tsin is quite right, I must find my mother; and of course I'm glad, because before I find her I shall see China."

On the next day Peter did everything for the last time: he was old enough now to be able to understand that. He took the cattle to the pasture by the riverside; he could ride now, on a quiet chestnut mare whose foal ran alongside her. She seemed to Peter the loveliest horse of them all.

For the last time, together with his friends, he looked for the nests of the water birds in the reeds, found their eggs and sucked them. He listened to the call of the golden eagle which flew high over the cattle, and in the evening he went with Fatima to the spring to fetch water. He dipped his fingers into the dish from which they all ate; he drank kumiss, and through the hole in the tent he looked up to the stars.

Early next morning, kneeling for the last time beside Ibrahim on the prayer carpet, he prayed to Allah, the God of the Mohammedans.

Then Fu Tsin's camels knelt down and their riders climbed up. Ibrahim stood in front of the tent, crossed his hands over his heart and wished him sound arms and legs. On the back of one of the camels Peter's rucksack was bouncing around; his red cap lay on top, but he had grown out of everything else. His bear lay underneath the red cap. He hadn't bothered about him for a long time, because living animals were much nicer than this moth-eaten toy — which had belonged to the small child he no longer was. Fatima must have packed him.

The caravan route which they took to the east was always the same; two pairs of grass-grown wheel ruts, one toward the sunrise and one toward the sunset. Hills, single trees, salt lakes — and white grass which shone in the sunshine; in the spring the lakes had flooded the banks, and the salt had stuck to the grass and colored it. The air shimmered under the hot midday sun.

"I can see red mountains," Peter said, "I can see houses, and there's a town. Are we nearly there?"

Fu Tsin answered quietly: "Don't look there, child; the mirages are lies."

But then real mountains appeared on the horizon, red and white wavy lines covered by the desert dust.

"We're near the border," said Fu Tsin. "I'm going to pray to Buddha and to the souls of my ancestors that it will be possible to take you over the border without the guards noticing. You have no papers. Many stamps and seals and many written words are necessary when a per-

son, even a child, wants to go from one country to another."

Now the roads which had been empty all day long
were filled with travelers riding camels or horses. Even a
couple of shaky cars pushed and steamed their way over
the sandy road. The steppes had come to an end.

"It's time now that I hid you," said Fu Tsin. "Be as
patient as a lamb, as quiet as a mouse, as blind as a fish
and as obedient as the son of a Chinese."

He undid a bale containing a hand-woven Persian car-

pet, one of several which he had obtained during his
journey, and told Peter to creep inside. Then he wrapped
the carpet around him so cleverly that Peter could get
some air. He was now as well hidden as a butterfly chrys-
alis in a cocoon.

Then the carpet was loaded back on to the camel. The
light shone through the folds as Peter swayed about on
the camel's back. Among the many colors there was a
rich blue, like his mother's dress. He had thought nothing more about it since he had left his Russian mother,
and now it reminded him of home. He heard a strange
voice talking to Fu Tsin.

"Have you any smuggled goods which you are trying to
take over the border?"

"Perhaps a single silkworm," Fu Tsin laughed, "but
there are plenty of those in China, and you won't find
it."

"And where are you going?"

"Home," Fu Tsin said. "I'm going to give my wife,
Peach Blossom, that fine carpet which lies up there on
top."

"She will be pleased to have it," the stranger answered.

"Certainly she will," said Fu Tsin, and he added to
himself, "and when she has unwrapped it she will be surprised too."

The camel swayed slowly forward and the "silkworm"
lay safely inside his cocoon as they rode over the border.

PART TWO

PART TWO

10

The Middle Kingdom

A SMALL Chinese boy called Fu Ling was sitting beside his grandmother, the Taitai, the First Lady of the Fu household. He was holding an ivory fan in his hand which he waved to and fro to keep her cool, because she was very fat and even on this mild autumn day was sweating.

As Fu Ling waved the fan to and fro he looked through the wide-open door of the paneled room with the bamboo beams, out on to the cobbled courtyard in which his grandparents' house stood. He lived with his mother, Red Jade, in another house of the same size; paths and gateways of red lacquer beams held the two houses together.

There was a pool of goldfish with a little bridge over it. It was only an ornament, since one could just as quickly go around the pond; but then everything was small and neat in Fu's house. Neatest of all were Grandmother's feet, and her name was just as soft and lovely: Peach Blossom. As the Chinese boy, who went to a modern school, looked at his grandmother's face he thought that she rather resembled a ripe peach, but he didn't mention it. A Chinese child is brought up to have great respect for age.

Fu Ling looked small beside her huge body sitting in an ivory carved chair, wrapped up in yellow silk. He wore a narrow-fitting blue cotton jacket over very full trousers.

He said: "Honored Grandmother, may I ask you something?"

"Ask," said the Taitai, and even though she loved her grandson there was no expression in her face.

"O Wise Grandmother, why are your feet so small that they won't carry you?"

"Once upon a time I was as light on them as a peach blossom in the wind," the grandmother replied.

"Why didn't they grow?"

"They were bound up when I was a child. Because of my little feet your grandfather, Fu Tsin, made me the First Lady of the house."

"But my mother has big feet, and my sister Puan has feet just like us boys."

"The times have passed when people understood about beauty. Since the Revolution many of the good old customs have changed. Our beautiful China will not be seen again. And will they rise, all those who died in the civil war? Your father, for example, my eldest son Fu Wang? When your grandfather, Fu Tsin, and I die there will be only you to pray before our shrine, and to pour wine on the earth, and to decorate our grave with flowers."

"Honored Grandmother, why don't I have a brother?" The old lady sighed for the third time.

"Don't make me sad, Ling. I told you, your father died in the civil war. Because of that you have no brother, even though Fu's house is big enough to hold ten grandsons."

"I would have liked a brother," Ling whispered. "Puan is only a girl with a fringe on her forehead, and her games are boring. She watches the crickets chirp in the bamboo cage when I want to fly my kite. And she plays her flute when I want to swim in the lake, and she never comes with me on the junk when Grandfather's merchandise is being loaded. Puan —"

"It's a good thing that Puan is so quiet and modest; I don't like these modern girls who are as wild as boys. But listen, Grandson Fu Ling — you're going to have a brother."

Ling almost let his fan fall. Grandmother Peach Blossom caught it with her little birdlike hand and held it before her face and laughed softly.

"But you've just told me why I can't have a brother," Fu Ling said, astonished.

"Don't interrupt when I'm trying to explain something. Your grandfather has written a letter saying he has already crossed the western border, and even the moun-

tains are behind him. Now he's riding along the river,
and either today or tomorrow he'll arrive. Wu read me
his letter."

"But I could have read it to you," Ling said and
slapped his chest.

"It is not allowed," his grandmother answered with
dignity. "Grandfather's letters don't belong in the hands
of boys."

"And my brother?"

"Don't be impatient!" his grandmother said, but she
smiled quietly behind her fan. "He smuggled him over
the frontier in a carpet."

"Is he so little?" said Fu Ling, disappointed.

"If you've patience, my First Grandson, you'll see
whether he's small or big."

Ling didn't need to be patient for long. In front of the
door which led onto the street they heard a commotion
— and the sound of voices. An old servant came into the
room and bowed before his mistress, his wrinkled yellow
face shining. "The Old Master is coming."

The Taitai said to Fu Ling:

"You may remain beside me, but don't move and
don't show any excitement about your grandfather's return. It is not correct. And if you like your new brother,
wait a little while and then go up to him and bow."

"In school we shake hands with the new boys."

"Your teacher studied abroad," Grandmother said
scornfully. Then a second servant came into the room; he

was a young man and his mistress did not expect the same respect from him as from the old servant; he did not bow but merely stood aside for the master to enter.

Ling wanted to run and meet him, but his grandmother sat near him and he had to obey her. She held the fan stiffly in her hand and sat very straight and still in her chair. Now her small eyes were alive and she beamed with joy. Fu Tsin was a big man who, in spite of his age, carried himself well. He still had on his traveling clothes, which he had worn in the trading tents of the west, and so he looked like a stranger to Ling.

Grandfather walked happily toward the Taitai, bowed before her, and waited with a serious face for his grandson to perform the customary greeting which was owed him as the master of the house and his father's father. Ling was a little hurried, and he didn't give such careful, well-phrased answers as his grandfather might have expected. While his grandfather was chatting with him, Ling's eyes searched the room for his brother; perhaps somewhere behind the servants, who had just come in to greet his grandfather, there was a boy, so small that one could have hidden him in a carpet to bring him over the frontier.

"My grandson Ling is impatient," Fu Tsin said. "He's never learned the art of patience," but he laughed as he said it and stroked Ling's smooth black hair.

"Where's my brother?" Ling asked. Grandfather laughed so loudly that he shook.

"I took him to your mother, Red Jade. She's going to wash and dress him. It was necessary! She's going to put on one of your tunics, because he can't stay as he was when he was running around in the Kirghiz steppes."

Ling looked astonished.

"A real Kirghiz? A boy from the Kirghiz steppes, where the shepherds with the fat-tailed sheep live, and the great droves of horses? You've often told me about it! Has there been a civil war there too?"

"In the Kirghiz steppes there's peace; nowhere in the world is it so peaceful — sheep, horses and shepherds! No, the strange child comes from a long way off in the west. In his own country it's now midday; here it's already evening."

"Do Chinese live there too?" Ling asked, and waited in fear for the reply. If the child was a foreigner then he didn't want anything to do with him.

"Oh, no! China is the Middle Kingdom. Foreigners live on the frontiers of the world. The child is German."

"I've never heard about them," Ling said shortly. "I don't want a foreigner for my brother."

"The war has destroyed his town and has taken away his mother. He himself was a prisoner of the Russians. Now he's looking for his mother and had gotten as far as the Kirghiz steppes. Since he won't find her there, I brought him here."

"Is his mother in China then?"

"Of course not, my silly grandson! And you appear to

have a very hard heart if you can't be friendly to a child who is looking for his mother. I brought him with me in order to try to find a way for him to reach home more quickly."

Now the Taitai roused herself.

"The teachers of wisdom, who brought us up, demand generosity toward everyone, and especially toward the guest who lives in our house. Why shouldn't a foreign child who is unhappy be your friend?"

11

Peter and

His Chinese Mother

Iт was very quiet in the room. Outside the doorway to the courtyard there came the soft noise of sandals on the parquet floor, and Fu Ling's mother, Red Jade, entered. She had put on a red silk brocade dress with colored flowers to honor her father-in-law. Above the dress her ebony hair shone. She was holding the little foreigner by the hand.

He was as big as Fu Ling and was wearing one of his blue tunics. It was too short in the arms and came only to his wrists. He tripped on the threshold, looking down laughingly at Fu Ling's sandals which were loose on his feet. His face was deeply tanned, and he had a very untidy mop of fair hair; his clear blue eyes were open and carefree.

Fu Ling shrank back. He had never seen anyone so ugly. So this was the foreign child, a German . . . ! And in spite of Grandmother's kindly warning he felt a hatred

welling up inside him. Already he had been taught in school to hate and distrust foreigners.

Peter looked at Fu Ling; he wanted to run to him, but Red Jade held his hand fast. Unwaveringly the blue eyes stared into the brown eyes of the Chinese boy and twinkled with delight. And then, suddenly, it seemed to Fu Ling that he really wasn't ugly — quite the opposite; he was one of the most beautiful little boys he had ever seen. Puzzled, he looked away. Red Jade came nearer. She bowed in front of the Taitai, and then in front of Fu Tsin, and then she pushed the strange child in front of the Taitai and let go of his hand.

He seemed a little undecided, but he held out his hand and said something to the Taitai which Fu Ling couldn't understand. It was: "Are your arms well? Are your legs well?"

Contrary to Chinese custom, Grandfather laughed. Fu Ling was horrified; he, himself, would never have dared to touch his honored grandmother unless she allowed it. But to his surprise she also laughed, took the child's hand between her two fat ones with the clawlike nails. She looked at her husband and said thoughtfully: "How can he possibly know? He has so much to learn!"

Fu Tsin said in Russian to the child: "Tell us your name!" and his eyes looked on happily as the child repeated something which sounded to the Chinese like a rasping hiss.

"Peter Reisiger, five years old, Ten Middle Road." He

was now eight, but as he had never heard a word of German since his travels began and did not realize how many years had passed, his little verse remained unchanged.

Behind him Peter heard giggling. He looked around to where the servants were standing, grinning and smiling in a friendly way.

Fu Tsin said, "We'll teach him our customs. We have lost much since the Revolution and our manners may be old-fashioned but we need not lose those too. Show him the kotow, Ling."

Ling threw himself on his knees and bowed his body so low that he touched the ground with his shoulders. Three times he repeated his deep bow. Then he stood up and went to one side.

Fu Tsin asked Peter to repeat it, and with his supple body he was able to do it gracefully. If it hadn't been for his blond hair above his Chinese tunic it could have been a Chinese who lay on the floor and made an exemplary obeisance three times before the Taitai.

"These foreigners are terribly clever," the servants whispered. With a red face Peter stood up and looked toward the friendly smiling face of the old lady, who nodded to him and with this movement accepted him into Fu's household. Peter began to be embarrassed because of their amusement. He understood quickly that he would have to be careful; he would do many things wrong. Everything was quite different from what he'd learned and done up to now.

He looked shyly around, but had no idea that this shyness made them like him. He met Fu Ling's look and his
courage returned as he walked over and stood beside him.

"Do you want to be my brother?"

Of course Ling didn't understand him, so they stood
dumbly side by side. They were almost the same height,
but Ling was not so sturdily built. Fu Tsin looked ap-
provingly at the two boys, the black and the fair hair, the
brown and the blue eyes — the two strangely assorted
brothers.

They were sitting in Red Jade's house around the dining table during the evening meal: Red Jade, the old
nurse Brokat, whose face was very creased, and the three
children, Ling, Puan and Peter Reisiger. He sat between
brother and sister, and they were too polite to look at how
uneasily he used the two chopsticks, and how difficult it
was to bring the dry rice up to his mouth without losing
half of it.

It really was difficult. He would never learn! He looked
with astonishment at the way Puan's little yellow fingers
managed the sticks, which she held together in her right
hand. With them she helped herself to pieces of meat
and soaked them in the yellow curry sauce, and not a
drop fell on her yellow dress or on the table, whereas all
around Peter's bowl it looked like a pigsty.

Red Jade laughed kindly; then she stood up, placed the

two sticks properly between Peter's big red fingers, and it became easier for him to hold them.

When he had been with the Kirghiz he had put his fingers into the bowl, and that was a great deal easier! And he wondered sadly if he would ever get enough to eat here. The people not only spoke like birds, they ate like them too. But his new family was very patient and old Brokat helped him, so that at last he had emptied his bowl and was full.

Afterward, the three children went out into the courtyard. Puan glided with soundless steps over the parquet floor. In the moonlight, which shone over the courtyard and the low buildings, her yellow dress shimmered like a flower and her black hair with the fringe shone like lacquer. She was a charming child.

She talked constantly, in a singsong voice, and urgently repeated certain words so Peter could understand better what she meant. She put her hand in the pond and caught a slippery fish, from which the water dropped like pearls. She let him go and repeated the word which she wanted Peter to understand. She sped away to a room and came back with a little cage in which a cricket sat rubbing its hind legs together. A silvery chirping filled the yard; it was a sad sound.

So Peter learned the Chinese for "cricket," "madonna lily," "moon," "red," "gateway" and "fish."

And then they went into Grandfather's courtyard. He

learned the words "Taitai," "old gentleman," "mother,"
"house" and "yard," and also the words for "civil war."

At the words "civil war," Fu Ling, who had behaved
as quietly as a Chinese boy should, became a different
person. With wild gestures he explained that his father
had fought in the civil war and had been killed. He
waved his arms in the air as if he carried a flag; he pulled
out a sword; he held a rifle, took aim and made a noise
with his tongue. He choked, twisted around, shouted,
and then sank to the ground staring at Peter, and his eyes
were black with hatred, but not of Peter.

Oh yes, Peter understood him. He also knew about
war, and if here in China war had killed a father, it had
taken from him his mother and his country. He told
them about it with one word; it was the word they used
for Red Jade, but he meant the fair woman in the blue,
flowery silk dress. They managed to understand each
other and become friends the first evening.

Then Brokat appeared in the red doorway and called
them to bed.

On the next afternoon, when Ling and Puan had returned from school, they were allowed to show their new
brother the town. It was a town of bridges and canals
because the neighborhood suffered from the flooding of
the great river which flowed past in the distance. Just beside their own house they had to cross the first wooden
bridge. Behind them on the planks they could hear the
footsteps of the old servant whom Fu Tsin had sent with

them. Ling, who once outside the house was loud and
wild, decided to shake him off.

"Here's some money, Old Pu; go to the merchant
who's sitting at the other end of the bridge and buy
something from him that our second brother can give to
the Taitai. Be quick and we'll wait for you."

Pu knew that he was being deceived, but he loved the
boy, so turning his back on the children, he started a
twittering conversation with the merchant. The children
tiptoed away quickly.

When they got into the town, in the bustle of the narrow streets, archways and alleys, Peter's eyes, which were
used to the open spaces of the steppes, were almost
blinded; and his ears took time to become accustomed to
the many noises. In the shopping streets the children
were pushed and tossed like leaves on a river. And it was
now that Peter noticed for the first time that every race
has its own smells. Out of the tearooms was wafted the
smell of strange spices; it rose from the great copper ket-
tles, and mingled with the rolling stench of rubbish in
the gutters.

Above all this were waves of unceasing murmur, whispering and noise. Rickshas rattled past, the naked feet
of the coolies sounded lightly on the flagstones. People
who were pressing tightly against each other gossiped,
scolded, sang and laughed — all this sounded to Peter
like some sort of queer music.

Lovely Chinese ladies went past them, their faces

powdered yellow and their hair shining like lacquer, just as Puan's did. In front of a silversmith's shop a ragged old beggar woman crouched with her jacket open. She was warming herself in the afternoon sun. On her back she had a small baby, and in her hand a paper bag with dirty scraps which she had collected from the garbage cans. With her stick she was poking around, looking for the best pieces to eat.

The children went into a little general store. Rolls of paper for writing and painting hung from the ceiling; dusty ivory toys, and green jade, and bowls made of red lacquer and black ebony lay around everywhere.

Fu Ling behaved importantly, handled everything and began to bargain. But before he could decide what he wanted, the shop was suddenly full of people who crowded around the three children, gazing at Peter as if he were a strange animal.

A little girl pressed her way through the crowd, and out of blackberry eyes she stared into the blue ones. Then she lifted her hand and touched Peter's red hand. Peter took it away and the child began to chatter. Peter stood quite still and took no notice. In the Kirghiz steppes he had caught wild foals with a lasso and had ridden on the fat-tailed rams. But this was much more difficult — and he didn't know what to do.

Even Fu Ling was helpless. He called the shop owner and cried to him in a high-pitched voice above the noise of the crowd, but the Chinese shrugged his shoulders and

looked at the strange child with hatred. What did he
want here? Puan stood close to Peter and began to cry.

Peter did the best he could; he laid a hand on Puan's
shoulder and looked laughingly at the little girl's inquisitive eyes. He waited for something to happen.

Suddenly the door opened and Pu came in. He had
followed the children — merely pretending to be deceived. He only needed to mention Fu Tsin's name:
"These are Fu Tsin's grandchildren," and immediately
the shopkeeper bowed, then pushed the crowd apart.

"The foreign child also belongs to Fu Tsin. He's looking for his mother because the war has parted them. This
child suffers in the same way as our children."

With whispering and comments one or two women
showed their pity. The shopkeeper put his hand in his
bag and fished out an ivory monkey which he handed to
Peter. With open arms he pushed the inquisitive crowd
out and in a second the shop was empty. Then Pu took
Puan by the hand and led the children home.

12
Goodbye Again

ONE day when Ling and Puan were still at school Fu Tsin took Peter with him into his office.

"Before you leave us you're going to see the most precious thing in China. My clerk, Wu, is going to show you what a work of art our handwriting is."

Peter wasn't particularly interested in the writing because he couldn't write. What mattered was that he had learned that he was to leave.

"Why must I go away?" he asked sadly. Grandfather Fu Tsin patted him on the head.

"Ling and Puan love you like a brother, and the Taitai and I would like to keep you here forever, but have you forgotten that you have a mother?"

"When must I go? And will you come with me?" Peter asked shyly.

"I'm sorry, but you cannot travel with me this time," Fu Tsin answered. "In a few weeks a business friend will visit me and he may be able to take you with him."

Peter's heart began to beat faster. The sorrow of parting and the thrill of adventure struggled inside him, but in the end the joy of knowing that this long journey had not yet come to an end, and that it would lead him to his mother, was uppermost. After all those years she had become like a blue shadow, but now he began to remember her again; with shining eyes Peter walked behind Fu Tsin into the office.

In the middle was a white porcelain stove with logs burning in it. An old man sat close to it. He was wearing a dark blue tunic and both the man and his tunic looked gray and dusty, but Fu Tsin bowed politely.

"I bring you my second grandson, respected Wu; show him the old writing and how beautifully you paint the letters."

Old Wu stood up stiffly, bowed, and thanked Fu for the honor shown him, only a poor writer. There were hundreds of thousands of signs, he said, but owing to his bad memory he could only remember fifty thousand.

"Show him how we write," Grandfather said, and Wu went to a desk, put a brush into the little pot of color, pointed it carefully and with his ivory-white hand painted a sign on the edge of the page.

"He's writing the word '*tschi*,' meaning 'tooth,' " Fu Tsin said thoughtfully.

Peter could recognize the mouth which Wu had painted on the paper; it was four-cornered but the lips were clearly parted from each other, and above and beneath there were four pointed teeth.

"Is it so easy?" Peter asked.

"So *easy!*" Wu laughed. "Each of the hundred thousand signs can be changed by adding one or two brush lines, or leaving them out, and then they mean something different. Now I'll write a tree."

And there was the tree, a short line, another line for the earth and underneath three roots.

"*Now* see how easy it is!" Wu said.

"It's *very* difficult," Peter sighed. "Perhaps if I stayed here . . ."

"I've already explained why that isn't possible," Fu Tsin told him patiently.

They returned together through the courtyard, but now it all looked rather different; the carved wooden figures under the roofs were not there just for decoration — they meant something; the manner in which the creeper was arranged around the panel, the choice of colors, in fact all the friendly politeness here was ancient and full of meaning.

"When you reach home," Fu Tsin said cheerfully, "you must tell your father that you've been in the Middle Kingdom and that in spite of the wars and the changes that have come with the new leaders, much of its ancient wisdom will never die."

Several weeks passed before the merchant arrived. Meanwhile winter had come; the heavy rains had filled the canals in the town with yellow streams. In Fu's house everyone froze, and in all the rooms porcelain stoves were brought in and were fed with wood and rice straw. The

Taitai put on one garment after another, and warmed her tiny feet in a little clay stove in which tiny balls of coal gave out a soft heat. Often Peter had to hold one of her hands because her old fingers had become so stiff.

Huayu, the merchant, came at last. He was a broad, heavy man who wore Western clothes. His trousers were stiff on his legs, his leather shoes made such a noise that everyone jumped when he came in; he laughed loudly when he was happy, with his mouth wide open, and he said exactly what he thought.

"Hasn't my friend Fu Tsin made a mistake in bringing this child so far east? Now we must see how we can get him out of it."

Huayu held Peter between his knees, looked at him from his head to his feet, and spoke to Fu Tsin about the possibility of his return home. Peter hated to be held like that. He didn't like Huayu, but Huayu had a strong hand and held firmly to what he had taken hold of.

"If I take him with my ships down to the sea it would become more and more dangerous every day, because the further east, the more unsettled the country is. One never knows what might happen; robber bands are to be found wherever it's lonely. And on the coast he would probably run into a new war."

He then made a suggestion which Fu Tsin accepted. But the Taitai said softly, "You want to send him to the south? But there are the terrible mountains of the Himalayas which are so high that only the Gods live there, since they're not afraid of snow and ice! And the tigers! And the snow leopards! And the bald-necked vultures! How can a mere child travel south?" she grumbled slowly.

"He's not going alone," Huayu said dryly. "My caravan driver knows the passes over the mountains, in both summer and in winter. I'm preparing now for a journey to India; when I go I will take Peter with me."

And so Peter was to wait until Huayu came again, which would be in the spring. But in the spring the great river overflowed, bringing down the melted snow from the mountains.

The streets in the town were covered with water; the river had flooded the peasants' rice fields so that only the tops of the green blades of rice could be seen.

"Can you see the peasants' houses — over there in the water?" Fu Tsin's voice wavered with pity. "The people are very poor and have only one mud room, and now that will disappear. Can you see the people on the roof and the water buffalo standing right up to its knees in the waves? If the water doesn't go down soon everything will be lost."

"And when it goes down . . . ?" Peter asked.

"Then they'll be even poorer than they were. They will have lost their rice fields for this year, and the buffaloes won't even manage to find grass; they'll have to be slaughtered so they don't starve. And next year the men won't be able to plow their fields because the buffaloes are dead."

"But you could fetch them and the buffalo too! There's plenty of room in our house."

"For these people, yes," Fu Tsin answered thoughtfully. "But it's like that the whole length of the river. Yu and Yun, water and clouds, are more powerful than people. One must have patience and overcome one's misfortunes."

Peter felt indignant. If something is wrong one must change it. Suddenly he felt that the Chinese were strangers, so quiet about their misfortunes. Even at night he dreamed of the shouts of the drowning people and the cries of the water buffalo which stood with its feet in the water and would have to be slaughtered in the morning.

But the next morning everything was different. The water began to subside. It left behind a slimy deposit which lay like good manure on the fields, and the people who lived on the riverbanks were happy to plow and sow again.

At last Mr. Huayu let them know of his arrival. Fu Tsin said: "Tomorrow or the day after he will come to fetch you. Today I shall take you and Ling to the temple, because if you haven't been there then you've never really been in China."

The temple stood on a hill with steps leading to it. A veranda all the way around supported a roof over the in-

ner room. The roof turned up at the edges, and in spite
of its weight it looked as light as a tent blown by the
wind.

Ivory, lacquer, ebony — wonderful carvings were inside. Just as it had in Russia, Peter's heart suddenly con-
tracted; this was the holy place of a nation. Fu Tsin knelt
in front of the shrine and bowed, then Ling went on his
knees, and Peter did the same. He was only a guest, while
Fu Tsin and Ling were paying respects to the ancestors
of Fu's house.

On their return they saw that Huayu had already arrived, filled the house with noise, and had even made the
Taitai laugh. She sat in her chair and rocked happily
backwards and forwards. She kept her mouth shut and
shook with mirth. Beside her was Red Jade, beautiful
and quiet as usual, holding a fan in front of her face. She
went a few steps to meet Peter as the three returned
from the temple. She was like a mother to him and it was
hard for her to give him up.

At their evening meal he was allowed to sit between
her and Huayu. He was even given a glass of rice wine,
which Ling was also allowed to drink.

The rice wine tasted good but painful. It ran warmly
down Peter's throat and, it seemed, right into his heart.
Affection for these good people mingled with homesickness for the fair woman in the blue silk dress who was the
reason for this long search. Huayu sat squarely on a silk

cushion and laughed loudly, "The little stranger is drunk! And now he's beginning to cry!"

Peter felt ashamed because he knew that in China one hid one's feelings. He would never succeed in becoming a real Chinese! It was no use — he just had to cry — and Fu Ling clung to him and cried too, and Red Jade had tears in her eyes, all because of the rice wine.

Red Jade sounded her gong and the servant Pu came in and took both children to bed. And then Peter saw that his old rucksack was ready and that the bear was sitting on top. After all the gentle beauty he had experienced here, it looked rather fat and ugly. Ling and Puan had stared at it and now he understood why. Ah, but it was his bear, that had gone through everything with him and knew as much as he did. He held it tightly, and feeling both happy and unhappy, quickly fell asleep.

13

The Journey to Tibet Begins

Huayu's junk went upstream toward the mountains. He wanted to reach the caravan road leading to Tibet. The river had sunk a little between its banks, but it was still filled with flood water. The coolies had a hard job on the towpath. They were clustered together on the rope and their sweating bodies pulled the junk along on its journey up the mountain river. All day their monotonous singsong accompanied their work.

The junk was a flat wooden ship with a place in the stern for the little room which held Huayu's and Peter's beds.

All day, Peter stood at the side and watched the mountains going past. He felt sorry for the hard-working coolies.

"The poor men! Couldn't you use a horse? There are so many horses in the Kirghiz steppes!"

"Coolies are cheaper," Huayu said, and his face looked ugly and unkind. "They have done the hardest work for thousands of years for a copper penny and a handful of rice. Why should I worry! I only deal in silk and cotton, and occasionally smuggle opium and children over the border. What Buddha wishes takes place without my help."

"Buddha?"

"In Fu Tsin's house they honor their ancestors and obey the wisdom of Confucius. Wait till you come to Tibet, and then you can see Buddha."

Peter said thoughtfully: "You can't see Allah; the Kirghiz pray to him on a carpet. And many holy people were painted on the golden pictures in Russia, but God is invisible."

Huayu said: "Buddha has many faces. He can be a beggar, a child, or a golden image; and the highest man in Tibet, the Dalai Lama, is Buddha too." Now Huayu looked neither ugly nor unkind. Above his Western clothes his face was as ancient and secretive as all the others in China.

The coolies had let go their ropes when it was evening. They squatted gossiping on the bank, and with their chopsticks ate their rice from clay bowls, happy because Buddha wanted it so. Huaya, on the other hand, ate a heavy meal which the cook had prepared under the awning.

As Peter ate he stopped questioning. He lay down beside Huayu on the junk's deck and the huge night sky with its many stars was spread out above him. The moon

cast a silver light over the round curve of the mountains
which were asleep, like unknown animals or gods in the
night.

Huayu pulled out a long pipe, put a yellow ball of opium in it and smoked. Gradually his face took on a blissful look, and he lay there with open eyes and dreamed. The poison of the opium took him a long way from Peter, coolies, bales of silk and Gods. His powerless body lay there with hands shaking.

"Huayu!" Peter said, but he got no answer. He began to be afraid. The night was very dark, and on the banks of the river the coolies were pressed close together, asleep.

China was terrifying when Fu Tsin wasn't there, or the gay Taitai, Red Jade, Ling and dear little Puan.

Peter shook with fear as light, naked feet slid over the planks. Then he recognized the cook, who squatted down beside him. He looked thoughtfully at his master Huayu, now insensible from the opium, and gazed quietly at the strange child. The cook knew that Buddha might also be a small child, and it was much better if there were someone to look after him when his master had made himself so ill and when there were so many rogues about.

From his master Huayu, who was himself a rogue, the cook stole whenever he could, and thought it his right. But the child must be allowed to sleep quietly. As soon as Peter had shut his eyes, the cook carried him to his bed under the awning, away from the "river spirits" which are not good for children in the night.

On the next day they reached the end of their river

journey. The mountains on each side parted to make a wide valley where the river broadened into a lake. Thousands of junks were anchored here, laden with merchandise.

The rest-house, where Huayu and Peter had to wait until the caravan was ready for its journey, lay close to the anchorage, so no travelers could easily escape the fat landlord. Such an innkeeper knows at once if a man is rich or poor. He bowed again and again in front of Huayu. Then he saw the child, and at once his gaze became sharp and cunning. Yellow hair! White skin! A foreign child, and nowhere was there a foreigner to whom it could belong.

"Sometimes traveling strangers honor my house," he said with the politeness which he thought necessary to a rich man, "but they have never brought a child with them. Where has the honored Huayu found this child? Will he sell him?"

"Fu Tsin, the silk merchant, gave him to me. The boy is going with me to Tibet and from there across India and home. He's looking for his mother." He noticed the landlord's cunning look. Li, the landlord, laughed slyly when he heard the name of the rich Fu Tsin. The cook came to stand near Peter, held his hand and listened.

"Does the honored Huayu really think that the child will survive this dangerous journey? In Tibet either the sandstorms, the snow, or the vultures will eat him up; in

India it'll be snakes, tigers or the plague. And he will never find his mother. Leave him here and at least he'll remain alive. What do you want for him? Two camels? A good horse for your caravan? I want a boy who'll encourage travelers to come to my house. He's a rare bird! A strong, good-looking child!"

Huayu listened with his head on one side, then he met the cook's gaze and laughed loudly and happily.

"If I hadn't been Fu Tsin's guest, then perhaps I would have accepted your offer, so that the child could be spared a dangerous journey. But it is Fu Tsin's wish that he should go home. He's richer than I and has a long arm, and I swore by my ancestors that the child should come to no harm."

The landlord grumbled loudly and threw angry glances at Peter, and then turned away. It was obvious he would do no business here.

"Come inside, honored Huayu, and we'll smoke a pipe together."

The cook held Peter's hand more firmly.

"Come away! Li is a knave, but I'm your friend, and Huayu must be too, but only because Fu Tsin is behind you. Tonight you'll sleep in my bed and I'll watch over you. I'm not going to let you out of my sight until you're really on the road to Tibet."

That night the cook covered Peter with his own padded cotton blanket, sat down beside him and watched over his sleep. Meanwhile, the crescent moon passed over Peter's bed and over China — like a little ship in the night. It was looking down on other countries besides China, where Peter Reisiger lay sleeping soundly before he traveled further to find his mother.

14

Welcome by Monks and Vultures

How quickly the world seems to change when one rides a horse! Peter no longer knew if days or weeks had gone by since he had left Li's rest-house behind him — and with it China, the Middle Kingdom.

"What am I going to do with you?" Huayu asked in a bad mood on the day of departure. "We don't ride on camels like Fu Tsin, where one can always put a child up behind; the little Tibetan ponies are more dangerous. Look at them! Are you afraid?" The Tibetan caravan drivers had brought their ponies up to Li's rest-house. They wore no saddles and had only one rein, which was fastened around the lower jaw.

"I'll ride," Peter replied delightedly, and he took the rein out of the Tibetan's hand and sprang up on the pony. He pressed his thighs around the pony's belly and the pony shook its untidy mane. Shouting with joy, Peter galloped off. That was exactly what he'd been longing for.

The cook, who had been looking after him like a mother, wrung his hands. Huayu slapped his thighs and laughed.

During the early days all Peter's muscles ached from riding, and in the evenings when they found a rest-house, or had to put up tents because there was no inn on the lonely road, he fell asleep dead tired. All night long he slept dreamlessly between Tibetan caravan drivers and Chinese coolies, and close to the loud snoring of Huayu, of whom he was no longer afraid. Huayu realized he could make good use of this boy, and it was for his own benefit that he took care of him.

Peter was all over the place, often where Huayu couldn't be. He rode at the head of the caravan near the leader, a tall wide-shouldered man who wore a bearskin cape and carried a long stick with a flag to show who he was. He talked cheerfully with this extraordinary child, who looked like a ghost and understood as much about horses as a man. And as their talk was about horses, they understood each other very quickly — because all over the world horsemen talk about the same things, whether it's in Chinese, Russian or Tibetan.

Behind them the mules, with Huayu's rolls of silk and wool, swayed as they walked. Now and then one of them stopped, put his head down and appeared to remember that his father was a donkey. The coolies pulled at his halter, the Tibetans cracked their yak whips, but the mule protested shrilly and stubbornly refused to move.

"Tschu!" shouted Peter, and seized its mouth, as he had learned to do from the Kirghiz. The animal gave in and the whole caravan moved on. Huayu beamed.

"I'll keep you with me always, Peter Reisiger, and I'll treat you well!"

"But I want to go home!"

The mountains through which they were riding became wilder, with crags and deep gullies, bare and lonely valleys. They met fewer caravans and rarely came to a rest-house or a hut in the evening. It was cold and the air was thin. The horses climbed the mountain passes in single file. Somewhere in the distance was Tibet. The whole day long, huge birds had flown over the caravan, sweeping so low that their pointed wings almost touched the riders. The horses shied, they walked much more quickly, their coats white with sweat. Everyone bent his head away from the terrible birds.

"They're vultures," the caravan leader said respectfully, "birds of death," and fingering his amulet he murmured a prayer.

Peter couldn't understand him, but he felt that the country through which he had ridden so happily lay under the shadow of these birds. He rode back to Huayu.

"Yes," Huayu said, "the vultures are birds of death. Have you forgotten the Taitai and how afraid she was of vultures?"

Yes, of course he remembered Peach Blossom! He could still hear her: "The snow and ice will eat him up when he goes to Tibet, or the snow leopards or those dreadful vultures over the Himalayas!" That's what she'd

said, and Huayu had laughed at her; but he wasn't laughing now.

"How can the Tibetans bury their dead if the land is
frozen most of the year? Instead, they carry the bodies up
a mountain and the vultures come and devour them."

Peter shivered. He certainly didn't like the idea of being devoured by a vulture! He felt very much alive — and
was quite aware how wonderful it was to be alive. Then
suddenly his horror was gone and he became inquisitive.
"Do they eat the bones as well?" he asked.

"Oh!" Huayu laughed. "You got over it quickly! And
you'll see what can be made out of people's bones! You'll
soon meet the begging monks, and you'll see how they
wear them around their necks carved into prayer beads,
or as amulets, which are supposed to prevent the evil
spell of bad spirits who live in the valleys and the rocks.
Just wait and see."

Suddenly Peter had become quite white under his sun-
tanned skin.

"The Taitai was quite right, they're really dreadful
birds!"

"But the Tibetans don't think so," Huayu answered.
"They believe that all animals, and vultures as well, are
holy, because Buddha could be reborn in any of them."

"Buddha? You promised me that I should see him
when I reached Tibet."

"You never learned patience in China," Huayu
laughed. "Perhaps you almost stood on him just now:

there's an ant running away. Or you might see him in the wild sheep over there, or in the yaks in Bachtal."

"Is Buddha there?"

"I didn't say that he was there. But he could be," Huayu replied in an undertone.

"I thought he was made of gold?"

"Yes, he's also made of gold; wait until you see him."

With this to brood over Peter rode back to the head of the train.

They came to the top of the pass. The biting wind whistled and snow lay around, covering many heaps of stones in which sticks and flags had been stuck; they were the only things in all this loneliness which showed that people had once been here.

The caravan stopped and the Tibetans jumped down from their horses, which, shivering, turned their backs to the wind and with drooping heads, stood still and waited.

The riders gathered white stones and each of them put one on each of the heaps. Last of all the leader of the caravan put his stick in and tied a colored cloth to it, and then threw himself on the ground and prayed. The other Tibetans did the same. The Chinese lay down in front of the little mound of stones and said prayers as if they were Buddhists.

Of them all only Peter stood there on his strong legs. He felt slightly ashamed, and bent down and did the same. As he was bowing he didn't know whether he was praying to Mohammed or to Confucius in China, or if perhaps Buddha was there, invisibly, in front of him. The whole wide open space seemed like a temple.

He heard the sound of wings and looked up. A huge vulture flew down to the body of a dead horse that had been left behind by an earlier caravan.

It was dreadfully cold! Where in the world had they come to! The Taitai had said only the Gods lived up here. Peter wanted to live with people and not with the Gods! Then his rather frightened glance fell on the glittering white of a huge mountaintop which rose toward heaven in the distance. Nearby was a plateau with overhanging rocks, and on the top of it were houses. Where there were houses there were people — suddenly the loneliness didn't seem quite so dreadful.

"Who lives there?" Peter asked hopefully.

"The lamas," Huayu answered, "and naturally they already know of our caravan. They've sent out their beggars."

"And who are the lamas?" asked Peter.

"The monks who live here. But here they call them lamas."

And sure enough, on the next pass they met a begging lama; a huge, rough man dried out by the sun, the wind and the cold, whose eyes burned in a shaven head. He had his prayer beads made out of white bones hanging over his red robe, and Peter couldn't take his eyes off them. He knew quite well what they were.

The lama bowed in front of them, opened his mouth

wide and stuck out his tongue. In his hand he held an
empty bowl. Peter forgot the Gods and the vultures. He
simply stood there and laughed loudly; but a hand pulled
him back — Huayu shook him: "You must never laugh
at something you don't understand. This is a holy man
who prays, fasts and begs. Were you laughing because he
put his tongue out? That is a sign of his respect. Do you
want him to curse us?"

The lama was standing in front of Peter, looking at
him out of his deep eyes. Peter shivered suddenly. Then
the lama put his bony hand on the boy's head, and in the
middle of the cold wilderness, a sudden feeling of
warmth and protection went through him.

The caravan leader filled the begging bowl with corns
of barley, Huayu threw a coin into it, and even the
coolies gave a few grains of rice or small coins which are
used in China. The lama accepted everything as if he had
a right to it.

"*Om mani padme hum.* . . ."

"Is he saying thank you?"

"Oh no, he's praying," answered Huayu. "The words
mean 'Holy jewel in the lotus blossom,' and they mean
Buddha. All the pilgrims, all the begging lamas and
priests say it unceasingly. The whole of Tibet is filled
with this prayer."

"*Om mani padme hum,*" Peter murmured. They
sounded like magic words which he must know in order

to understand what was happening in this extraordinary country.

Since they had come over the pass they had been leading their horses by the reins up the mountainside. The animals picked their way up the slippery path and went forward slowly.

"If a horse can't carry his rider up the pass he isn't a horse — if a rider doesn't lead his horse up a pass he isn't a rider," the leader roared when he saw that Peter intended to remain on his pony. Ashamed, Peter dismounted. The way led around a rock, and suddenly they were surrounded by a crowd of boys who were no bigger than Peter, and, with their red robes and their shaven heads, were obviously *lamas*.

They saw Peter, laughed, crowded around his pony, jumped backwards when an old lama called, stuck their tongues out, bowed and begged.

"But I've got nothing," Peter said. "I'm a child like you."

They came nearer and pulled his pony's tail so that the animal kicked. They took the reins out of Peter's hand, felt his clothes and stared at his yellow hair. They became more and more troublesome.

"Huayu!" Peter shouted, but he had disappeared up the pathway. The last pack-pony had already gained the corner; the children now had Peter alone, and they laughed as the old teacher looked on.

"*Om mani padme hum!*" Peter cried out, not knowing what else to do. The children let him go and the old man gave him his reins back, put his hand on his head and blessed him.

Suddenly they disappeared like ghosts, and there, up ahead, was the caravan, and there was Huayu. Peter, quite out of breath, reached him at last.

"A good thing you've caught up," Huayu said. "The Khampas are coming."

The Khampas turned out to be wild-looking people. They gathered in small groups and plundered pilgrims and nomad villages and lived from their robberies. They had guns on their shoulders and circled angrily around the caravan. When they saw the leader take a similar gun from his saddle, and saw that Huayu wore a pistol on his belt, they went off. But Peter couldn't forget the horrible look on their faces when they had seen him.

That night they slept in a village composed of a few mud huts. They had no windows, only a hole in the roof and an open doorway. The next day the mules were to be exchanged for yaks.

The villagers had come forward to greet them; one of them, a friendly woman, took Peter by the hand, pushing her own children away from the fire of yak dung which was burning in the hut. She made Peter a bed from yak skins, gave him yak milk to drink, and yak meat to eat. The meat tasted bitter and was very fat.

She was a mother, and even if they couldn't speak one word to each other, it was lovely just to lie quite still in her hut and forget all about vultures, lamas, Khampas and icy mountaintops.

15

Danger All Around

Huayu's caravan was on its way very early the next morning, because yaks go much more slowly than mules. Their lowing woke Peter up and he saw a man come into the room. He took no notice of the strange child, but began to eat the tsampa porridge made of barley meal which his wife had put before him. During the night he had helped to load up the yaks for Huayu's caravan, and now he was tired and hungry. He swallowed loudly and his wife laughed at him.

Then the doorway darkened once more — it was the only way that daylight could come into the hut — and a similar man came in, almost the image of the first one. Perhaps the woman had two husbands? This one was greeted just as respectfully by the woman, who gave him his tsampa porridge.

Once he turned around to look at Peter and said quietly: "The little stranger had better hurry," then returned to his bowl and continued eating.

The woman came up to Peter's couch and made it clear to him that they were waiting for him. He understood her, and although he would rather have stayed here, he stood up and looked around to see if he might wash himself. But the woman had no idea what he wanted; he pretended to spit in his hands, rubbed them together and over his face, but no — washing didn't appear to be customary here. The children who stood around also looked as if they knew nothing about it. But they were happy, and after this night in the hut with a mother Peter felt happy too.

He went past the two men, who behaved as if he weren't there, and the woman followed him.

In the doorway he said: "Thank you very much. You're all very kind to me." But how was the mother supposed to understand? Then he thought hard and said: "*Om mani padme hum,*" and this time he got some tsampa porridge. The men stood up, bowed deeply, put out their tongues and pushed their bowls toward him. Without waiting, Peter sat down and ate everything. Then they took him to Huayu who was standing among the yaks.

The yaks stood with their heads hanging, snuffling through their bare noses. They were heavy, short-legged animals with very hairy coats, and so much hair on their legs that it hung down to their knees. Their horns were spread wide and turned upward.

The children with whom Peter had slept ran happily in and out, gathering the valuable manure which was lying on the ground. Peter began to help them, but

Huayu suddenly shouted: "Now stop it! What will the yak drivers think, what will the coolies think, what's your host, who's already shown you so much respect, going to think of you?"

He laughed as the woman came with a rather dirty towel for Peter to wipe his fingers, and she laughed too; and the children laughed and danced around them. Even the woman's two husbands turned away smiling. The yak drivers joined in, and the coolies, and the leader of the caravan, and through the bright Tibetan morning air their laughter reached up toward the summit of the mountains.

What a happy place Tibet was, and how amusingly this early morning ride began! How gloomily it was to end!

The yaks strolled along the path and soon the horses overtook them and drew a long way ahead. Huayu rode beside Peter and said to him:

"I've watched you during our long journey, and you're a good boy. Wouldn't you rather stay with me, travel and see the world with me?"

"I want to go home. The children in the mud hut have a mother, and I've got one too. Fu Tsin wanted me to go home to her."

"Fu Tsin is far away! I could *make* you stay. Without me you can go no further."

He was still quite kind, but a threatening tone had come into his voice and reminded Peter of Li.

"I know," Peter answered shyly.

"Well then! Think about it. I would rather you did it willingly — we shall understand each other better later on."

"Of course," Peter said.

"We are now coming to the Red Valley, and there you can show that you're a real man. The Tibetans are afraid of the valley because great storms hang over it all the year round. Particles of dust swirl around in the air in red clouds so people and animals breathe with difficulty. The Tibetans say it's the spirits who live there. When I'm in the middle of it then I think they're probably right. At this moment, of course, I know that it's the wind blowing dust down from the mountains, and that only the weather is to blame for it."

A shiver went down Peter's spine. He had just been so happy, and now Huayu threatened him and, at the same time, expected that he would be braver than even the grown-ups.

"Bother! Now the praying begins!" Huayu swore.

A sudden cloud of dust swept toward them from the entrance to the valley and covered them in a second, filling their eyes and noses. They had stopped in front of a huge, golden image. The drivers and the caravan leader lay down on their stomachs before it, praying to Buddha, the guardian of the valley, to protect them from the spirits.

So this was Buddha, the first God Peter had ever seen! He must be very powerful; he was covered in gold; everything was gold. The naked shoulders, chest, stomach, arms, and the quietly clasped hands, the widely placed knees, the crossed legs upon which he sat — all were gold!

His face was of extraordinary nobility, severity and kindness. The eyes stared unmovingly over the Tibetan mountains which belonged to him. Peter couldn't do other than jump down from his horse, bow as deeply as ever in his life and repeat the prayer words which he knew. *"Om mani padme hum!"*

Buddha would certainly know what he meant by that. He wanted to go home! He wanted to find his mother!

Huayu stood up and swore at the yak drivers while the leader of the caravan cracked his whip. Against their will the yaks began to walk, the horses snorted and their riders had to spur them on — the caravan had entered the Red Valley.

The earlier dust storm had been only a small sample of what was to come. Now the whole valley was covered with the red clouds through which the travelers could see nothing at all, not even the mountains on each side of their path. The air howled, whined and whistled. Then it seemed to take a deep breath and the storm died down. It had covered them all in a red cloak. Then everything began again, louder and wilder than before.

During the pause Huayu's voice could be heard trying to keep the caravan together. If a yak is afraid he lowers his head to the ground and comes at you with his horns, bellowing loudly ready to fight; or, he turns around, throws off his load and tries to run away. The horses reared, their manes flying in the air and their hoofs beating on the rocky ground.

The riders had dismounted; they tried to hold their animals by the short reins, but they were pulled all over the place. At the same time they had to hold an arm in front of their faces as the dust stung like a thousand pinpricks.

"Peter, Peter!" Huayu shrieked.

The respected Huayu must have gone mad. There must be spirits; Huayu could say what he liked but he obviously believed in them himself. And was Peter supposed to help him? A shudder of fear went through his body and conveyed itself to the pony. Up to this moment Peter had managed to hold it. Now it galloped off down the valley as though the spirits were behind it. The caravan and its noise died away behind. Suddenly the wind dropped, but the pony galloped on and on and Peter had to go with it.

They galloped over a plain where a lake frozen in the coldness of the coming night appeared to dance past them. Quite near it a hot spring came out of the earth and shot clouds of white steam into the air. A distant hill appeared with the setting sun behind it. On it was a fortress which shone like gold through the dusk. The pony galloped straight on toward it.

A man was leaning against a yellow stone post by the roadside. He raised his hand and achieved what nothing else had been able to do — he stopped the pony. It was shaking all over, covered in a white lather. The man came near and Peter recognized him. It was the begging lama who laid his hand on Peter's head yesterday and had looked at him through his deep eyes.

"There you are," said the man, speaking in Chinese. "I've been waiting for you."

Peter answered: "How did you know that I was coming?"

"It was arranged," he replied quietly. "The God King, the Dalai Lama, wants to see you. There are secrets in Tibet which I can't explain to you. Come with me!"

He took Peter's hand and led him toward the gold-crowned fortress.

It was strange — this lama commanded great respect yet he seemed familiar to Peter, as if he had always known him.

"You have come from a long way off," he said as they walked along, Peter holding the pony's reins.

"Yes, I have, Peter Reisiger, Ten Middle Road. My mother —"

"I know," said the lama, "you want to go back to her.

But first you'll see the Dalai Lama, the Living Buddha.
It's allowed to few people. But since he's only a boy, he's
just as inquisitive as a boy. He'll like you."

Peter's head was spinning. The God King, the Living
Buddha — a boy! It was very difficult to understand.

"You can't really understand. Whenever a Dalai Lama
dies Buddha looks for a new body. He enters a new-born
child, and this child is the new God King, if only we can
find him. He might be found in a palace or in a hut, with
a merchant or with a yak driver. Who knows Buddha's
will! For years the lamas search for him; they travel
through the whole of Tibet until they are certain."

"Don't they make mistakes? Is it really Buddha whom
they've found?"

"A mistake isn't possible," the lama replied with cer-
tainty. "The lamas recognize the signs. The child has
small marks on his forehead, and his ears stand out, and
his hands have lines which only the God King's have.
The Dalai Lama ran toward the lamas although he was
only two years old when they found him."

"And then you take the little boy away from his
mother?"

"Of course! He's brought to the Potala, here to the
fortress of the kings. He has lamas and abbots for his
teachers. Wherever his feet have trodden becomes holy,
and whatever he has used is holy. Once a year many
thousands of people pass by his throne, bringing gold and

gifts and receiving his blessing; the Dalai Lama touches their heads with a silk tassel."

"Has he anyone to play with? Friends, or parents?"

"His mother lives in a palace nearby and is allowed to see him. She was a poor peasant woman, but now he has raised her to a higher level."

"Oh, poor boy!" Peter sighed deeply. "I'm glad Buddha didn't decide on me to be the God King of Tibet."

At this the lama laughed.

16
Peter and the Dalai Lama

THEY had now come nearer to the Lhasa town over
which the fortress, the shining and mighty Potala,
reigned. The turrets and towers of the holy city rose high
above them.

The road was full of lamas and merchants who were
going to Lhasa. Among them were pilgrims who had a
journey of years behind them because they had neither
ridden nor come on foot — they had measured the thou-
sand-mile journey with the length of their bodies, and
were still doing so. They stood up, walked to the place
where their heads had lain on the dusty road, threw
themselves down, and pulled their feet up behind them,
much like caterpillars. Then they stood up again, throwing a hungry glance toward the towers of the holy city
which was their life's goal, and so went slowly forward.

Peter felt a dread of the holy boy who demanded such
awful things — and who could not be really happy
either.

"How old is he, and what's he called? Everybody must
have a name."

"He's now fifteen years old," the lama answered. "And he no longer has his own name."

No ordinary name! thought Peter. No one to comfort him when he's afraid, no one to laugh with or to tease him; and probably he's not allowed to cry either.

"I shall say something friendly to him when I see him. Perhaps I could give him something," Peter decided.

"You'll give him a white silk scarf, like many others who come to him. We buy them in the bazaar in Lhasa."

"I've got no money," Peter said. The lama laughed.

"Look in your purse!"

And there were two pieces of Tibetan money! The lama must have put them in.

Peter asked, astonished, "Can you make magic? Do it again! Show me how you did it!" But with a stern face the lama went through the entrance to Lhasa and the guards bowed deeply.

The holy town, the forbidden city!

"Look around you," said the lama, "for only a few Europeans are allowed to enter."

The town was full of colorful crowds and didn't look a bit holy. The houses were several stories high and had many verandas and balconies; the shops touched each other. Dust lay on all the windowsills, was blown by the wind in clouds through the narrow alleyways. The gutters were dirty and smelled horribly.

But everyone was cheerful, moving about happily. Lamas in their red robes had gathered in small groups under the golden roofs of the many temples, blowing long trumpets or banging gongs. In their hands pilgrims turned prayer wheels which sounded a single note.

Peter and the lama tied up the pony at a pilgrims' rest-house. Peter settled his rucksack more comfortably on his back.

"Perhaps I have something I can give the boy, to make him really happy for once. Kolja has my train — but I do know of something!"

"You'll give him a scarf, just as I said. Come with me to the bazaar and we'll buy one."

People were crowding around the stalls in the bazaar; there were men of all the Asiatic peoples: Tibetans, Chinese, Cossacks — and there was a Kirghiz in his caftan and his tall cap with its green leather lining. Peter wanted to run up to him. He shouted loudly: "Are your arms well — are your legs well?" The Kirghiz jumped and stared at the child as if he were a ghost.

They looked for the scarf under hundreds of others which were laid out for sale; it was customary in Tibet to give one as a token of honor. They chose one made of the finest silk and several yards long.

"Now come along!" said Peter's companion. "Don't look around anymore. We'll go through the Jewel Garden in the Potala."

They went through a door in a wall into a large park, and then through a gateway into a garden where cages with parrots and songbirds rocked in the branches; they

passed elephants and a tame leopard, and a kennel with
long-maned dogs which cringed in front of the lama.

The high fortress walls of the Potala appeared in front
of them, doors opened and they went through dark pas-
sages with walls a foot thick. The cold air was stale and
musty like that of a prison.

Then they had to climb many stairs. Last of all they
came out on a flat roof which was surrounded by several
other golden roofs; the Dalai Lama lived here — they
had arrived!

A door opened into a small room which was lit by an
opening in the ceiling. Dark red covered the walls, and
golden lamps filled with butter burned on each side of a
throne hung with brocade.

A boy sat on the throne — no one dared to look at him
except Peter. Even the lama who had brought Peter low-
ered his gaze, for it is allowed to very few to gaze on the
Living Buddha.

Still holding the lama's hand, Peter, with a friendly air,
walked toward the throne of the God King. He did not
see the distrustful faces of the high priests who stood
beside the throne; nor the woman in heavy silk, smooth
black hair above her huge face, laughing gently because a
child was breaking all their customs. He saw only the
eyes of the boy king, which looked seriously into his own.

The lama pulled Peter down, knelt beside him and
with his forehead touched the ground before the Dalai
Lama. Peter made the deepest kotow of his life; but he

did it quickly, so anxious was he to look at this boy who
was a God.

It was quiet in the throne room; the blue eyes and the
brown ones met. In the blue eyes the wide world was
reflected: mountains, rivers, towns and steppes; men,
women, children and animals; adventures and dangers.
Of these the holy child, who was so strongly guarded,
knew nothing.

But he longed for it, and his eyes asked question after
question. And a light burned in them which Peter had
never seen before in human eyes.

"Give him the scarf," whispered the lama.

There was a slight delay: as Peter's rough hands
touched the delicate silk, he could hardly free himself of
it. When he looked up at the Dalai Lama, the Living

Buddha was laughing, just like any boy who was enjoying a visit. He bent and took the scarf from Peter.

Peter sighed with relief. It was really going wonderfully well. How lucky it was that Red Jade and the Taitai had taught him good manners.

"What did you say, please?" he asked politely, hearing the God King speaking to him. His voice was soft and quiet, a clear, unbroken child's voice that went up and down like a bird's song.

"The Dalai Lama wants to know your name," the lama translated.

"Peter Reisiger, five years old, Ten Middle Road," Peter said — so loudly that the lamas took a step back in horror.

But the Dalai Lama laughed. "Wouldn't you like to stay with me? You could go to the cloister school and you could learn, and pray with me. And you could tell me all about the world you've come from, and be my brother in the Potala and in my summer palace. We could be very happy." His eyes pleaded.

Peter pulled himself together. Now it was necessary to be brave!

"Unfortunately," he said with fear in his voice, "I can't stay. I'm looking for my mother."

With that he looked at the woman whose face shone with kindness. She must be the boy's mother; perhaps she could help him.

"He's looking for his mother," the lama translated unwillingly.

The woman drew near and her large yellow hands took him by the shoulders.

"If a child is looking for his mother, no one should stop him," she said sorrowfully. "Mother and child should always be together. My son shall bless you."

As light as a butterfly the hand of the Living Buddha was laid on Peter's head. The two were so close that they could hear each other breathe.

Then it occurred to him that he had forgotten to give the boy his bear, but now he was ashamed that he had even thought of it. He swallowed once or twice, took a deep breath and was Peter Reisiger once more, the brave young globe-trotter.

"Yes, of course, I must go home," he said and looked questioningly at the lama. "But how shall I do it?"

"I'll take you to a rest-house where I know a rich merchant who's going to India tomorrow; he'll take you with him," the lama said. "Now that the Dalai Lama has blessed you I know you will find your mother again."

Peter followed him confidently. His road led on, but he would come to the end of it, that was certain.

17

Lost in the Jungle

The bamboo bridge over the jungle river swayed slightly although no one moved it. A monkey jumped out of the roots of the mangrove trees, clambered up on the bridge, made itself fast with an arm and a leg and began to scream.

A boy came out of the undergrowth. He walked along the small path which led to the bridge, climbed up the bamboo ladder and stepped on the long bamboo poles which were bound together and made up the bridge. There was a handrail, but he didn't touch it; like a rope-dancer he put his arms out in order to balance himself.

He stood in the middle of the bridge like a huge strange bird and laughed aloud; in front of him sat the monkey and wouldn't budge. With its huge round eyes in its old child's face it looked at him and chattered quietly. The boy sat down in the middle of the bridge above the river, and swung his long legs over the water and waited.

The monkeys were used to people. Not far away was a Hindu village, and fishermen's huts stood here and there on the banks of the river. Dark-haired golden-faced children lived here, and whenever the monkeys wanted to, they played games with them.

But the child on the bridge was frighteningly different. He was dressed like an Indian; he wore a tunic and a cloth wound around his waist like that of the Hindu boys; he had a bright blue turban on his head. As the monkey pulled at the tunic, the child hit at the tiny black animal fingers with his large rough hand. The monkey ducked away, came boldly back and tried to touch the turban. But the boy pulled it off his head, and waved it happily to and fro. The bridge bounced and shook like the branch of a palm tree, but the monkey was used to that. Then, as he came back for another try, he saw something terrible.

The boy's hair was like that of an old man; it was as yellow as a banana, and his eyes were not black but blue. Worst of all, the cloth around his waist held an animal such as the monkey had never seen before; its coat was yellow with brown spots, like half-rotten banana. It was dirty and moth-eaten, with a round head and single blank, black button eye.

The boy saw the monkey's horrified look as he stared at the bear. He laughed even more loudly and held it out to the monkey. "Boo!" The monkey screamed loudly, and with wild leaps ran back to the jungle.

The boy stood up and crossed the bridge. He wanted to have a little walk while the Indian merchant Schek-

har, who had brought him from Tibet to India, com-
pleted his morning prayers with the other men of his caravan. He, Peter Reisiger, had bowed deeply three times
to the west just as he'd learned from the Kirghiz, Ibrahim. There was no prayer carpet as there was in the Kirghiz steppes, nor ancestors' shrine as there was in China,
nor golden statue of Buddha such as he had seen in
Tibet. And he had no inclination to let the river water
flow over his head as the Indians did; it was holy but the
water was dirty and filled with all sorts of little creatures.
Besides, it was much better when he went away while
they were praying.

All day long during the journey they were kind and
friendly, but he noticed that during their prayer hour and
at their holy washing they didn't care much for him. If
he touched one of them the man immediately washed his
hands, and they waved him as far away as they could.
Even his *shadow* was not allowed to touch them. But
here by the riverside it was cool and open; the tortoises
weren't bothered by his shadow, and he hoped the monkey would return. Instead Schekhar's deep voice sounded
from the depths of the mangroves:

"Peter, Peter! We must go on while it's still cool."

Schekhar was a good man, but Peter had no wish to
go.

"Just a little longer," he called, because he was enjoying himself.

Schekhar didn't wait — he preferred to bargain. He came up the path after Peter.

"Don't go any further," Schekhar said. "The jungle is dangerous. A bit further down we shall come to a ford over which the caravan can pass. You'll laugh to see how frightened the yaks are of the tortoises; they've never seen them in Tibet."

"No, there are none there," Peter replied in a friendly manner, and a sort of dizziness came over him for which the sun or the steamy jungle might have been responsible. Schekhar saw that Peter was slowly walking toward the other end of the bridge and tried to persuade him to return.

"Just one more day's travel, and then we shall have reached the railroad. You'll see —"

Peter didn't want to see. He didn't want to hear. That was all. He watched how Schekhar clumsily began to climb the bamboo ladder up to the bridge, and how he stood there undecidedly. Schekhar wasn't a brave man, although he had never shown any fear of the torrential mountain streams, the steep declines and the precipices of the Himalayas. He was used to the way and knew where it led; knowing it had made him a rich man. But this bridge, loosely put together, swinging above the holy tortoises and surrounded by the shrill cries of the monkeys, was something different.

"There are elephants and rhinoceros, wild buffaloes

and snakes over there in the grass jungle!" he shouted. "At this time of the morning the tiger is about — and it's possible that he's not yet made a kill and that he's hungry."

For a second Peter wavered, and Schekhar laughed with relief. The merchant stood at one end of the bridge and Peter at the other, and they both looked out across the countryside; on the right hand was the clear-cut edge of the jungle decorated with gaudy red and yellow flowers. It looked as if the jungle were standing in the water on the high stilts of its mangrove trees. On the left-hand side, like an ocean, was the unending grass plain, man-high bamboo canes, grass like swords.

The land spread out to the north, and forests crept up the sides of the rocky mountains through which they had just come — evergreen oaks, magnolias, rhododendrons and laurels. Above them lay a wide band of firs and birches. Their eyes looked higher still, at green mountains, naked rocks — and far away —

"Tschomolungma," the merchant said gaily.

He clasped his hands together and pressed them on his forehead as one does when praying. Far away, high in the sky like a cloud, rose the highest mountain in the world, ice-blue Tschomolungma, the Mother-Goddess of the world.

"Europeans," the merchant said, and seemed to imagine that Peter could hear him although the monkeys screamed disrespectfully. "Europeans have given her a

man's name; they call her 'Mount Everest.' But what is
worthy to be named in the same breath as the seat of the
Gods?"

There was no answer from across the bridge. For a
time the merchant remained deep in thought, and then
remembered that he had come to fetch Peter back. But
Peter had disappeared. Schekhar stared horrified at the
empty bridge; he tried to put a foot on the swaying poles,
but brought it quickly back. "Peter, Peter!"

The monkeys chattered and laughed like spectators at
a comedy. Their noise drowned his calls. It seemed to
Schekhar as if the grass moved on the other side, but it
might easily have been an animal coming through.

"I'll send Anil after him," he told himself; "he's strong
and bold and perhaps he can overtake him. If the boy
goes even a step off the path he'll never find his way
again. The lama in Lhasa entrusted me with him."

The path which led into the jungle gave way under
Peter's footsteps; the ground was boggy and Peter
jumped to one side to avoid the pool which appeared.
High reeds whose tops shook over his head covered him
with a cloud of yellow-gray pollen. A foot-long lizard
scrambled over his foot; he cried out, and his cry in the
warm damp jungle awakened a thousand other voices.
They twitted, shrieked, whistled, chirped, whispered and
purred.

Peter's heart beat so loudly that he could hear it, and

his head began to ache under the hot, oppressive sky which stretched like a burning roof above him.

Turn around, turn around! Schekhar had been right. Quicker, quicker, Peter! Go and find him! What a pity you didn't obey sooner!

"Schekhar, Schekhar!" and with a burning face he broke through the bamboo thicket he had accidentally entered. Where was the path? He had lost it — and he was old enough to know what that meant.

A wild trumpeting sounded through the jungle — once, twice — elephants! His heart jumped with fear; he froze in his tracks; his feet were as heavy as lead. He needed all his willpower to work his way through the undergrowth and perhaps, if it were possible, to find a way out of it.

Suddenly a huge butterfly flew toward him, alighted for a second on his head, flew away, and came back, fluttering with gentle wingbeats in front of him. And almost at once Peter discovered a small path which led through the thick stalks. The butterfly was a shimmering blue; what did it remind him of? Suddenly he thought of his mother. She seemed to laugh at him; she waved and beckoned.

"Mother, Mother!"

With soft steps she went in front of him, and changed every so often — sometimes a butterfly, sometimes a piece of blue silk, sometimes a sunbeam, a laugh or a bird's call. She was Mother and he was her child. She helped to get him out and no other person could have done so.

The path became wider, the grasses were fewer and the butterfly flew gently away into the air. Was it really his mother? For a second the fever left him and he looked around to see where he was. A little lake lay in a clearing, and over on the other side two elephants with a calf were trotting around it. Further away two huts lay behind a palisade, their reed roofs rising above it.

In the shade of a fig tree a man sat holding a gun. He looked up and saw the strange child coming toward him out of the jungle. The sun, now high in the sky, burned relentlessly down, and it seemed to Peter as if he would never reach the shade of the trees. He stumbled forward, hot arrows shooting through his eyes; he ran, tripped, pulled himself up and fell into the arms of the man. Then he knew nothing more.

18

Peter Is Lucky Again

As he awoke, Peter felt somebody rubbing his tired muscles with a nice-smelling ointment, then he saw a pair of black eyes looking at him.

He tried to laugh. A little girl in a rose-colored sari was leaning over him. She jumped back as soon as she saw that he was awake, and smiled kindly at him.

His head ached, and he discovered that it was bandaged with a thick cotton cloth. He shut his eyes.

When he opened them again the girl was standing by his bed, holding a jug of milk in her hand. She looked at him questioningly, then held the jug to his mouth with her small brown fingers and he greedily drank the cool fresh milk.

After that he was really awake. He found himself in a little room, where a mango tree in front of the window spread its green shade over the house.

The girl put the jug down, and standing by his bed pointed a finger at her chest and said: "Sasi."

So she was Sasi, and it seemed to Peter that if all the people were as nice as she was, he would enjoy himself here. He made a little movement as if he wanted to bow, and whispered the verse, which had accompanied him across the world: "Peter Reisiger, five years old, Ten Middle Road."

"Oho!" a man's voice speaking German laughed. "He's awake, and he's German, but he's certainly not five years old. Good morning Peter, twelve years old, at present in the village of Tshundipur in Bengal, India. When you feel better you'll have to tell me how you got into the jungle."

Peter's mother would have said: "No he's just past eleven, it's simply that he's very big and strong. . . ." But his mother, and the butterfly, had disappeared once more, and the rather odd German, which the Indian had learned in Germany many years ago, was difficult for Peter to understand. He had been too small to know his own language properly when he lost his mother, but now these strange words sounded a bit like home, and he began to feel better almost at once. The man came to his bedside, and Peter saw it was the same man who had caught him in his arms under the fig tree. He had brought him at once to the hut of the simple Hindu people with whom he stayed when he hunted in the jungle.

"You're lucky, Peter," the man said, "I intended leaving today. I don't like shooting elephants when they've got a calf with them. But now I'll wait a day or two until your arms and legs have recovered."

Of course he didn't know why Peter laughed so loudly when he said that, because obviously he'd never lived with the Kirghiz as Peter had.

Sasi's mother came into the room. She was a pretty young woman with a heavy black knot of hair, and she stood very straight. She had painted the red mark of a married woman on her forehead. She looked down when she saw the elegant sahib sitting near the strange child's bed, and waited at the door until he had gone.

Then she sat down beside Peter's bed herself and was as relaxed and carefree as her little daughter. She made a spoon out of some bread, dipped it in a bowl of bamboo shoots and rice and fed Peter.

Peter got well quickly. In a few days he was able to get up and sit with Sasi in the shade of the mango tree near the house. He had a new turban, which he used as a scarf around his shoulders as soon as the evenings grew cool. But when he began to run about he wound it around his head; he'd learned to know the Indian sun!

At first a few of the village boys looked at him in surprise, and then decided to tease him. They put a lizard on his shoulder and waited for him to scream, but as he laughed and found it amusing they soon became friends. Peter played with them on the lake shore, rode on a bamboo raft in the shade of the bank and caught fish in his bare hands.

In the evening clouds of smoke came from fires in the

cow sheds. This was necessary to protect the holy animals from the mosquitoes. From a distance, out of the huts of the untouchables, the poorest of all Hindu people, came the shrill one-tone song of their evening rest.

Sasi sat beside Peter, and in the small amount of Hindustani which she had taught him, tried to make it clear to him that she was eight years old, and that her mother had married her father when she was eight years old and had come to live with him when she was fourteen. And Sasi and Peter would have to marry soon if they didn't want to be too old.

"I only wish I knew if your caste is on a level with mine. Because otherwise it would be extremely unfortunate for our children."

A caste: that was the position into which people were born, and which they could never change — a man could never be other than what he was. The caste system was very rigid; a marriage between people of two different castes was impossible, unless the higher one came down.

"Anyway I've got to move on," Peter answered coldly. But he was just a bit sorry that she couldn't be his wife. Somebody behind them laughed gently. It was the sahib; Sasi sprang up and stood shyly to one side while Peter turned to speak to him.

The short evening soon turned into night. The thousand voices of the jungle awoke; across the sky a bright moon sailed past, and the southern cross gleamed above

them. The scent from strange flowers was almost suffo-
cating.

"Now come to bed," the sahib told Peter, "because
tomorrow we have to leave. India is a large country, and
we have a long journey before us."

19

Beside the Ganges

THE jungle was still filled with night sounds when at last the sahib and Peter were ready to leave the hut. They had to wait for the hour when the tiger is full and returns home, and the elephant has gone his own way, and the snakes have slipped back into their holes in the earth.

Sasi stood in front of Peter and put a dewy wreath of white blooms around his neck. She was decorating her nicest guest, who had nearly become her husband; she herself wore in her hair a golden flower which had opened the day before and had an overpowering scent.

They traveled downriver past the forests and the grass jungle until they came to a small railroad station. A train was getting up steam, and would perhaps leave tomorrow or the day after. The carriages were packed full of people who were waiting patiently.

The sahib, however, unlike most Indians, became impatient. He was not waiting for the train but for a motor car which at last appeared. It shone red like a jungle

flower under the tropical sun; it was decorated with a
swan's breast and golden feathers. The swan's neck was
bent back and glittering eyes had been put in its head.

It rolled toward them on its thick rubber tires and, to
make up for its extreme quietness, let out a three-toned
sound from its horn. Peter felt that anyone who could
ride in such a car must be the luckiest of persons.

"Whose is it?" he asked in astonishment.

"Why, ours! Come, get in; we're late already."

They got in. The seats were covered with golden brocade and Peter worried about his dirty hands and feet.

The sahib laughed. "Drive on, Ratan," he ordered the
driver. "In Benares we'll have to buy him European
clothes; we mustn't let the maharani see him like this."

Seeing that Peter looked puzzled he explained that the
maharani was his wife. He himself was the maharaja.
Most of these princes of India were still immensely rich,
but their power was growing less as modern ideas took
the place of old ones.

The driver touched things on the dashboard; music
came from — the body, the board, the upholstery, or
from the sky? The music played a happy tune and went
to Peter's heart. Excitedly he opened his eyes wide and
said: "Where does it come from?" It seemed that in India everything was possible.

"Have you never heard a car radio? How long have you
been on your journey?"

"All my life," Peter answered. "Only much earlier

Mother was there. The poor God King of Tibet should have a radio; he gets so bored in his golden Potala."

"What are you talking about? And what do you know about the Heavenly Child?"

"I was there with him; he's very nice but I'm sorry for him."

"I too," said the maharaja from the depths of his soul. "Neither he nor I will be able to enjoy our present lives much longer. The future is almost upon us. You children will experience it."

He sat there looking at the boy at his side. At the straight forehead and the mouth which was no longer as soft as that of a child, but already showed strength and willpower. He had long limbs and his hands were full of scars. His language was a queer mixture of Russian, Chinese, Kirghiz, Tibetan and now Hindustani; even German, his childhood language, was coming back to him, since his protector spoke it better than he did.

For a child coming from the loneliness of the jungle the next day in Benares was a complete puzzle. They left the car and walked into the alleys of the old town, which led up steps to the Ganges. Thousands of pilgrims were going their way, and they had only one goal: the water of the holy river which would make them pure.

They passed mysterious-looking temples, and from out of their darkness they heard gongs beat, and from the shadows the many-sided faces of the Gods threatened them.

A town of tents and booths had been built up beside
the riverbank, and the smell of all the food and the
overpowering smell of cows poured over them in the
heat, which in the early morning was already almost un-
bearable. They were bothered by merchants selling sou-
venirs and beggars running along beside them. Sick people lay beside the path and showed their open wounds in
order to get pity, and everywhere cows were lying around
chewing the cud. Both the rich and the poor pressed toward the river, and starving people crawled along by the
walls of the houses.

The great Ganges flowed wide and quietly over a bed
of clay. The steps which led to it were full of people who
were shouting and crying. They kissed the holy steps, and
penitents knelt, saying their prayers aloud in clear voices,
to Siva or one of the other gods of India of which there
are very many.

Some of the pilgrims had painted their naked breasts,
and wore two crossed white marks on their foreheads.
Others had a round blood-red fire-mark on their brows. It
was the sign of Kali, the wife of Siva. The beggars' eyes
were shut, and they lifted skinny arms in the air, remain-
ing like this for days on end, and living only on the
grains of rice which a sympathetic pilgrim might put on
their haggard lips.

Frightened by the scenes around him, Peter caught the
maharaja's hand.

"Do I have to kneel down? Must I kiss the ground? Must I really bathe in that dirty river?"

But his companion, the elegant maharaja, didn't reply. He put a hand over Peter's mouth and walked with him down the steps. He put his own feet as far as the ankles in the holy water and sprayed himself with a few drops. Peter did the same. The water of the Ganges flowed around his feet and his face was touched by it as if it were a blessing. They didn't go as far in as the mass of people who were dancing, swimming and diving in the middle of the river, letting the muddy water run over their hair and bodies.

At last the man at his side spoke. He looked happy and had a warm light in his eyes.

"The human soul must always struggle for existence. A single life is not sufficient for it. It dirties the soul with bondage and dust, with sins and pains, but the water of the Ganges, which comes down from the glaciers of the Himalayas and from the throne of the Gods, washes everything away. Now it's time for us to go."

They went back to the upper town and drove along the shopping street to a big store. When they left it Peter had become a European: he was wearing a silk shirt, white linen trousers, a rice-straw hat, and under his arm he carried a parcel of similar garments, because his shirt was already sticking to him and would soon have to be changed. The Indian clothes had been much more com-

fortable! He looked both proud and unhappy. The shirt
was tight around his hot neck, and the waistband of the
trousers seemed so tight around his middle that he had
to hold in his breath.

"You'll soon get used to it! I've heard some news: a
Mr. Peperkorn, a Dutchman, who is coming to visit me,
will take you back with him. You can't go home to Germany dressed like an Indian!"

They drove on and on. Gradually the countryside
changed into broad parklike country. Now they were
driving along a wide avenue of palms, and the car had to
stop as a train of elephants came toward them, carrying
heavy trees in their trunks.

"These are working elephants," the maharaja said.
"They're building a bridge. In an hour or two we shall be
home. But first I'll show you the most beautiful thing we
have in India. I want you to think kindly of India later
on."

They turned off the road and came to a lake which

gleamed like molten silver between its green banks. Behind it stood a huge building of marble and gold. Steps led down to the lake, and at the corners of the walls which surrounded it there were tall turrets standing up against the blue sky. They were decorated with figures. Was it a temple or a palace?

"A shrine," the maharaja said thoughtfully, "which one of the emperors built for his wife several hundred years ago. Can you see the marble tower, as red as the evening sky, as fine as lace? Can you feel that this is a place of peace and love?"

"No," Peter said honestly. "I felt it much more when I was with Sasi." Then he held his breath, but the maharaja laughed kindly.

"I'd forgotten that you're not an Indian child."

They drove on until a high wall appeared with a wide moat in front of it, and the car rolled soundlessly over a bridge and through a gateway into the courtyard of the palace.

Servants appeared on all sides, and arranged themselves in a file on the steps to greet their master. The man at the head stood as straight and proudly as if he himself were a prince. The men behind him were arranged in order of importance, and last of all there was a dirty little boy, whose glittering black eyes looked out from under an enormous turban. He opened them wide as he saw Peter jump out of the car behind his master. He couldn't stand still for excitement, and while all the

others were making a deep bow he looked at Peter and
made signs with his fingers. Peter smiled at him, and the
boy laughed back, but the man at the head shouted,
"Kanti!" His voice was filled with anger, and Kanti
pulled himself together and made his bow.

That evening Peter ate with the maharaja in a great
dining room. There were servants for every dish, and the
plates they put in front of him were made of silver and
gold; they handed him slices of bread so he could carry
the food to his mouth. This was much easier than trying
to eat with Chinese chopsticks!

The servants were sent out and the maharani came in.
She wore heavy gold ornaments decorated with jewels;
on her head and brow, a wide necklace and glittering
bracelets. Even on one of her ankles there glittered a gold
and jewel bracelet, but in spite of her rich adornment
Peter saw that her large dark eyes were very sad. Sasi's
mother had looked much happier in the jungle, and she
was poor.

"We want you to be happy here," the maharani said
kindly, "until Mr. Peperkorn comes to take you away
with him. How can a mother be so careless as to lose such
a child?"

"It was the war," the maharaja answered gravely.

Peter was given a room which belonged entirely to
him; there was no glass in the windows, which were made
of stone latticework. There was a low bed over which a
mosquito net was draped, and an even lower table. It was

incredibly boring, and apart from that his headache, which he'd first had in the jungle, returned. Outside it began to rain.

He lay on his bed and stared at the ceiling. Even here, in a palace, spiders managed to crawl in through the windows, and if the servants hadn't removed them carefully he would have been glad of even their company.

At last during one of the pauses between the rainstorms the maharaja came and took him down to the stables. There were many elephants chained there, waving their trunks to and fro and flapping their ears. They held out their trunks toward the visitor, and Peter offered them pieces of sugar which they ate with pleased expressions.

Now they came to the horses, and Peter ran delightedly from one lovely animal to the other, patting them on their necks and caressing their soft noses.

"Can you ride?"

"Oh, may I?" And he was already sitting bareback on one of the horses. Taking hold of the gaily woven leather halter he went off on a wild gallop. The horse threw its head back and tried to unseat him, until it sensed the hand of an experienced rider.

The sky became dark and it would soon rain again. Kanti rushed up behind Peter and slapped him on the back, as one does with friends. Peter pretended not to

notice it, because almost at once the head servant
screamed from the courtyard.

"Kanti!"

"He belongs to the lowest caste, the untouchables,"
the maharaja told Peter. "I brought him to my court because I, like many others in India, wish to break this
caste system. But it is more difficult for the servants because everyone suspects those who are lower than they
are. If they weren't afraid of touching him, then Kanti
would feel the stick more often."

During the evening Kanti slipped secretly into Peter's
room and brought a couple of lizards out of his dirty
tunic. Peter's headache had disappeared. They squatted
together on the tiles and let the lizards run about, caught
them and let them run again over the colored tiles. After
that the two friends sat with their legs swinging over the
low marble windowsill and breathed in the soft night air.

"It smells in the kitchen," Kanti said, playing with his
bare toes. They were clean, because every day he washed
them in honor of his God, and in the same way his teeth
gleamed because he could say his morning prayers only
with a clean, fresh mouth.

"When the Russians cooked pork it also smelled,"
Peter informed him.

"Pooh, pork! That's dirty!"

"And what about beef?"

"Cows are holy things, and whoever eats them will become an outcast in the next life. My grandfather once held a cow's tail in his hand and that helped him to die peacefully."

Peter knew that one mustn't laugh about other people's customs, but he couldn't help it, he laughed now at the top of his voice. That was the end of their friendship.

Kanti said angrily: "I would as unwillingly touch that horrible animal on your bed as you would a cow's tail."

"It's a God which protects me," said Peter boldly.

At this Kanti laughed, but rather uncertainly. "He's got straw coming out of his hands, and his coat is as dirty as our dustbin, and his one eye —"

So Peter seized his bear, pushed it toward the boy and shouted, "Boo!"

Kanti screamed loudly, ran to the door and disappeared. He never returned.

Peter caught the lizards which were trying to climb up the wall, put them out the window, and was now lonelier than before.

Mr. Peperkorn, the Dutchman, had arrived, and the rains were almost over. Everything smelled fresh and clean outside. Mr. Peperkorn was a dry, sick man who was going on a long leave to Europe. He wore a white silk suit and a pith helmet, and in honor of him the maharaja was dressed in European clothes.

When he saw Peter, Mr. Peperkorn almost closed his eyes. He wasn't at all pleased that he was to have a child with him on this journey. The maharaja reassured him.

"It's not the child's fault, and he's quite good. But he's got to be taught European manners; he'll learn quickly."

Mr. Peperkorn was the right person to teach him. On the long journey home, how would he know how to eat and drink, when to be silent and when to talk, how to greet people and how to sit down?

Peter's heart stood still as he listened to them.

"We don't want his mother to have a rough, awkward boy when he reaches home," said the maharaja.

Mr. Peperkorn laughed peevishly and Peter thought to himself that it would be frightful.

20

The Extraordinary Mr. Peperkorn

Eᴠᴇʀ since Peter had been traveling with Mr. Peperkorn he felt as if he were bound hand and foot. It was
really terrible!

The sky was as blue as ever, and after the rains the
palms were such a bright shiny green that they looked as
if they were lacquered. The birds flying about were pretty,
and happy; but everything was boring because Mr. Peperkorn was boring.

During the entire time they were driving in the red car
over the gleaming white roads, past temples and shrines
made of marble and gold, Mr. Peperkorn sat with his
eyes closed, and the sweat ran down his parchment face.
Once they overtook a traveling Hindu family swinging
along on their camel. The woman had pulled her shoulder cloth over her head, and a little black-eyed girl stared
at Peter in the car from between the bundles fastened
between the camel's humps.

"Sasi, Sasi!" Peter shouted — But of course it wasn't
Sasi, and they were past very quickly. Mr. Peperkorn's
bony hand seized his belt and pulled him back on the

seat. He grumbled: "If you don't behave better than this
on the ship I shall put you off at the first port. You're not
the most important person here."

For a while he tried to sit as Mr. Peperkorn was sitting;
with his eyes closed and his open hands resting on his
knees. The wind rushed by him, the road sang under the
car and India went past them.

Peter couldn't put up with it for long. He wanted to
see and he wanted to enjoy himself. He opened his eyes
and met the driver's dark look in the little glass over the
windshield. The driver lifted his hand and waved to
Peter in the mirror.

Peter made a face at the driver as if he'd been Kanti,
and then the eyes disappeared from the mirror and once
more he was alone. He pulled out his bear in order to
have some company, but it was quite extraordinary how
the bear had changed during his world tour. It was no
longer a plaything — or was it that Peter couldn't play?
But in another way, he appeared so much more alive, a
quite secret bear, who knew more and understood more
than a boy could possibly know. Peter held him on his
knees and stared into the one-eyed grubby face as if he
were looking at him for the first time.

"It would be best if we threw that dirty beast away at
once," Mr. Peperkorn said. "You can't take that with you
on the ship."

Horrified, Peter pulled the bear to him and looked toward the little mirror to see if the Hindu could help

him, but Peter couldn't catch his eye. The car purred on, the miles disappeared under its wheels and the minutes of the bear's life were numbered.

Mr. Peperkorn said mockingly: "Nobody knows how old you are, but in any case such a big boy can't play with a toy bear!"

"He's not a toy," Peter tried to say, upset, but how could Mr. Peperkorn understand what the bear meant to

him — he, himself, had no idea why he simply had to keep him. And then suddenly the Indian's eyes looked at him out of the mirror. The Indian smiled at him, nodded and winked.

"May I ask the sahib to let me have the ugly little animal as a present for my son? Then the young sahib is free of him, and the big sahib need no longer be ashamed."

For a second Peter wavered, then again he saw the

black eyes looking at him, twinkling and laughing. Confidently he handed the bear over and the driver placed him under the seat.

They drove on through a flat swampy land and came to Bombay. A colorful mixture of people wandered here — the native dark-skinned people from India's hinterland, long-headed Persians, Arabs and Turks. And for the first time in his life Peter saw Englishmen. The British had ruled India for centuries and only recently had she become independent. They wandered along on their long legs, fair men with red faces, as if they were still the masters.

"Do I look as funny as the other Europeans?" Peter asked disappointedly. For so many years he had seen only Asiatics, who looked beautiful to him.

"Europeans funny!" Mr. Peperkorn roared, "Perhaps you find me funny too?"

"Yes," Peter replied, "very."

Then he saw how the red color flushed Mr. Peperkorn's thin skin and tried to explain to him: "So — so lonely — so unhappy."

Mr. Peperkorn drew a deep breath and turned to say what he thought of the boy, but suddenly he shut his mouth and his eyes were quite soft. He put a hand on Peter's shoulder.

"I expect I've been too far away from home far too long," he said quietly. This second of trust was quickly past. "But you must learn not to say everything that you think," he added.

"To the Dutch consulate, driver!" he called over the seat. "I want to try to get papers for this little European so he can go home!"

"Papers?" Peter asked in astonishment.

"Every person has to have a passport, which shows what he's called and where he's born, and how old he is — and many other things too."

"I didn't know," Peter said. "I'm Peter Reisiger, that's all; the rest of it isn't true anymore."

"Well, as long as I don't have to say that you're my son!"

"I *hope* not!" said Peter.

Mr. Peperkorn looked at him darkly. "You can wait down here. The Hindu seems to be your friend, and I don't want to have to apologize for you upstairs."

He disappeared into the narrow entrance to the big building, and Peter turned around and looked at the driver expectantly. Now something would happen!

The Hindu laughed, showing his white teeth, but his eyes remained serious. "Be quick! Who knows how long Mr. Peperkorn will be upstairs. Hide him in your ruck-sack."

Peter held his bear close to him. The driver helped him to open his sack; there was a shirt, a suit of camel hair wool, a pair of shoes and socks — and in between these Peter hid the one thing which he really owned in the whole world, the small bit of his native land that remained to him. Thoughtfully he looked at it as the driver closed the rucksack and put it back in the trunk.

"Must I really put on those thick clothes?" he asked sadly, as he thought of how heavy and warm they would be.

"Naturally," answered the driver, who seemed to know everything in the world, and whom Peter trusted blindly. "Someone told me that Germany is covered with snow all the year around; everything is white, and everything is cold."

"Yes, that's right," Peter said after thinking about it for some time. "The meadows were covered with snow when they were shooting over them. And Father sat behind a mountain of snow. He pulled me over, otherwise they would have hit me."

"Were you in the war then?" the Indian asked, startled.

"I think so."

They were sitting in the shade of the red car because the Indian sun filled the streets with a burning heat. Dark memories filled Peter's head.

"But the apple trees — apple trees were there too, and they were in bloom — when do they bloom then, in the middle of winter? And Mother —"

The Indian looked sympathetically at the strange child.

"How shall I find my home? I don't even know the name of the town, and there are so many towns in the world —" And the boy and the man sighed together over this puzzle.

Upstairs in the big building Mr. Peperkorn said to the consul, "Of course he must go home. I believe the Germans have a very good organization for finding people who were lost in the war. I can't do anything else but take him with me."

"Without a passport?" the consul observed. "We know you here, Mr. Peperkorn, your plantations and your cotton mills, and your wealth. But your money won't have the slightest effect upon the strict passport regulations. After all, what do you know about him?"

"He's a wonderful little fellow," Mr. Peperkorn said, to his own surprise; and in his eyes a warm light appeared. Then he laughed mockingly: "I've just discovered that I like him. I certainly shan't leave him here. I suppose I handle him rather badly, but I have to do that because he's half-wild!"

"Aren't you going to suffer for it? What have you undertaken? Here's a child, and you've no idea what he's like! A real wanderer — and how do you know if his parents can be traced? Hand him over to a children's home!"

"Never!" Mr. Peperkorn said energetically. "Please add his name to my passport as that of my son. He's

twelve years old — distinguishing marks? Oh yes, lines of
scars on his hands and — several languages."

The consul asked dryly: "Can he speak Dutch?"

"Not a single word," Mr. Peperkorn laughed, and took
the passport which was held out to him. He put it in his
pocket quickly as if he were afraid the consul would re-
gret his generosity.

21
Peter in Trouble

The *Wilhelmina* trumpeted like an elephant and growled dully like a jungle tiger. The last passengers were climbing up the gangway. Groaning and stiff, as if he had no joints, Mr. Peperkorn crept up and was pulled on board by some sailors; Peter jumped along laughingly behind him.

Behind them was the silhouette of the town bathed in the red of evening; the first lights had appeared and grew brighter like a glowing farewell.

Motorboats darted over the water like spiders, and the high dark sails of the Indian fishing boats clustered together as they came in from the sea in a small flotilla. Soon the night would descend very suddenly, and Mr. Peperkorn would have seen India for the last time. He shivered and seemed to be ill.

The ship was ready to leave when a car came racing down the pier, and a lady and a boy got out just in time to come aboard. The lady climbed the gangway carefully, while her son paid too much attention to his long white trousers. He and Peter stood and looked at each other.

The newcomer studied Peter's rough hair, his clothes which — even though they were new and made of the best Indian silk — hung untidily on his body. Then his gaze fell on the scarred hands.

"What an odd-looking boy," he said scornfully to his mother, and although Peter couldn't understand a word he noticed the scorn. Kanti, with his lizards and the dust in his turban, was nicer. This one looked so smooth and so empty.

Beside him Mr. Peperkorn suddenly came to life.

"Oh, dear madam!" he called and rushed up to the lady and kissed her hand. It was clear that they were old acquaintances. Mr. Peperkorn turned around: "You must meet my son, Peter. Come here, Peter!"

Peter stepped forward, took the hand offered him and kissed it. The lady quietly wiped the back of her hand and laughed politely.

"Ah, a gallant little cavalier! I didn't know you had a son!"

"Nor I," stammered Mr. Peperkorn, all mixed up. He now began to realize on what sort of adventure he'd embarked. The lady kindly overlooked his mistake.

"Come here, Edward! Greet Mr. Peperkorn's son. Shake hands — you'll soon be friends; then you won't be bored any longer."

But Edward didn't move: he ignored Peter's outstretched hand. "His nails are dirty."

It was true; his nails *were* dirty, and Peter himself

looked dirty. But as Mr. Peperkorn watched him standing there with his hand out, quite ready to be friends
with the conceited boy, he greatly preferred Peter.

Edward and Peter were to share a cabin, a tiny room
with two beds, and a marble washbasin.

Outside a gong was sounding; the same sound had
called the Chinese and the Indians to their prayers.

"Come on," Edward said, "dinner. Your father will be
very happy!"

It was a good thing Peter didn't understand him because apparently he meant something unpleasant. And
so Peter went down behind him, having no idea that his
misfortunes had already begun.

The ship began to get up steam and the passage leading from the cabin seemed to go up and down. In the
dining salon they discovered Mr. Peperkorn already at a
table with Edward's mother, looking impatiently toward the doorway.

Peter made his way between the tables and broke into
the middle of their conversation, until Mr. Peperkorn
seized him and made him sit down.

"You mustn't interrupt. Watch Edward and do exactly as he does, and then everything will be all right."

Of course it wasn't as easy as that; his napkin slipped
off his lap, and knives and forks were much more difficult
to hold than Chinese chopsticks; and it wasn't very easy
to know when one should use the knife and when the
fork.

Mr. Peperkorn grew red in the face and said apologetically, "I've had no time to teach him manners."

"In these things Edward is perfect," the lady answered. "Peter will learn from him quickly; we'll shut our eyes."

But they didn't shut their eyes — they all stared at him, even from the neighboring tables.

"A child of the wilds — a charming child — where on earth did Mr. Peperkorn find such a strange boy?"

Peter had never felt so ashamed in his life. He felt Edward's cold eyes looking at him, and he didn't take his gaze away as Peter looked down and began to swallow hard in order not to cry.

Edward laughed; so Peter was a crybaby! The first

thing a boy must learn is that he should discipline himself.

Edward's mother tried to excuse him. "Don't you feel
very well, Peter? Perhaps your father will take you to the
cabin and you can have a good sleep. Everything will be
better tomorrow."

"Nothing will be better tomorrow, and he's not my
father!" Peter said loudly, because his sobs had stuck in
his throat. Mr. Peperkorn jumped up and everything was
quiet around them. Then they went out of the salon together, just as the music began again.

"You'll stay here in your cabin until you've learned
how to eat and drink properly. Tomorrow the hairdresser
will come and give you a haircut like Edward's, with a
straight part; and the steward will have to wash your
clothes and — and — bother, boy! Why did you have to
tell them that I'm not your father? It's down in my passport, and that can't lie. What's going to become of you if
I'm *not* your father?"

"I've already got two fathers, one in Russia and one in
Germany," Peter said in a worried way.

"But you haven't got one on the Indian Ocean!" Mr.
Peperkorn shouted. That sounded like an angry remark;
he meant it affectionately, but how was Peter to know
that?

"Get into bed," Mr. Peperkorn said, opening the cabin
door and pushing Peter in. The door banged behind him.

On his way to the dining salon Mr. Peperkorn had noticed that the rolling of the ship had given him an odd feeling in his stomach; this upset with Peter made him feel even worse.

Peter saw at once that someone had unpacked his rucksack. The bed was turned back and at the foot of it the bear sat, staring insensibly at Peter out of his single eye. Neither of them had ever experienced anything like this before! Since there were no pajamas in Peter's rucksack, a pair of Edward's silk ones had been put on his bed — with the tips of his fingers Peter pushed them to the floor. He threw off all his clothes and crept just as he was, shaking, under the bedclothes. He pulled the bear to him, and sobbed so hard that he shook all over. The bear listened patiently to his crying.

"Now we're prisoners — just like the elephants in the stables, and Puan's cricket in its bamboo cage."

He put his face into the moth-eaten coat of the bear, and became quieter.

"We're not going to remain prisoners, I tell you, and I'll never be Mr. Peperkorn's son; and I'll not be an ape like Edward either. We'll run away from them!" When Edward came in he was fast asleep.

"Huh! He plays with a Teddy bear too," Edward said mockingly.

22

The Tall Indian

Next morning Peter dressed himself, and rinsed out his mouth, and cleaned his teeth to honor the God Siva just as the dirty Kanti had done. Then he bowed to the Mohammedan God in the direction in which he supposed that the sun would go down in the evening.

For the moment it lay shining on the waves which were dancing in front of the porthole, and above them was a piece of bright blue sky. The porthole went up and down, so that sometimes the water and sometimes the burning blue sky appeared. The rolling of the ship was lovely. Edward's best suit swung on the wall, and Edward rolled around uncomfortably in his bed, from one side to the other.

He had awakened at last, looking green, and he stared in astonishment, no longer so stuck-up, at the boy who seemed to be enjoying himself.

"Are you ill, Edward?"

But he turned away and didn't reply. He closed his eyes and sighed, then he jumped up suddenly, ran out in his silk pajamas and didn't return. Mr. Peperkorn didn't appear either, so when the gong sounded Peter went out into the passageway alone. But he didn't dare enter the dining salon. The door stood wide open, and the people who sat around the tables turned their heads, stopped eating, and stared at him. His stomach rumbled from hunger, but it seemed better not to go in.

The Captain came along and stood beside him. "You must be Mr. Peperkorn's son."

He spoke German and Peter liked him. He had smiling eyes and a white line on his forehead where the brim of his cap had been. He wiped off the sweat, holding his cap in his hand. "Hot, isn't it?"

"It was hotter in the jungle," Peter said.

"Oh, have you been there too? Would you like to come with me and tell me something about it? I've ordered breakfast for you in my cabin, and I'll sit there with you. Your father is ill; he asked me to look out for you."

"Mr. Peperkorn isn't my father."

The Captain laughed. "That got around already. I really don't know which of you two is the more to be pitied in this relationship, you or Mr. Peperkorn."

"I do!" Peter said decidedly.

In the Captain's cabin the fan was going, and the Captain lounged in his shirt-sleeves on the cool leather seat, looking on while Peter had breakfast. Peter left his spoon where it was beside his plate of porridge, took a piece of bread and, without making any crumbs, guided porridge, orange juice, milk, raisins and nuts into his mouth.

"You're well brought up," said the Captain. "Other countries, other customs; you seem to have learned quickly what other people do."

Peter's face shone. All his shyness and nervousness disappeared and everything was once more right with the world.

"Is Mr. Peperkorn going to die?"

"No, he's only being seasick. Some people are sick the entire time — until they've got firm ground under their feet again. And Edward will be no trouble to you either; he's exactly the same."

"But I've been lucky!" Peter observed, and they both laughed, because nobody is likely to die of seasickness.

"I've still got a little time; tell me about yourself."

So Peter began his story, stumblingly at first, and then more and more excitedly: what a wonderful world it was, and how kind all the people were whom he'd met; he had never starved and he had never been really afraid; and he was never entirely abandoned.

The Captain looked thoughtful. It was quite clear to him that this boy had come safe and sound across the world because of his own character. He wanted to protect him from Mr. Peperkorn.

"Mr. Peperkorn is down in the papers as your father," he said carefully, "and he'll have to stay that way because you can't go around without papers. But I'm on your side; run around the ship just as you like. I'm sure you won't do anything wrong."

Peter continued to sleep alone because Edward was being nursed by his mother. He had his meals with the Captain and made friends with some of the sailors. He was allowed to go down into the engine room, and he stood beside the navigator's charts and watched the movements of his electrical instruments.

The Captain had warned him: "You're not to go down between decks to the coolies and the Indians. They're tough men and different from your Indian and Chinese friends. We'll soon be in Africa and then we'll have to clean things up down there."

One day Peter saw Mr. Peperkorn. He was lying in a deck chair in the shade; he looked hopefully toward Peter when he was not being watched, but covered his face as if he had a toothache as soon as Peter said "Good morning" to him politely.

"We've lost a great deal of time, and you're just as wild as ever. The Captain knows nothing about children. Well, we shall have to make up for it when I'm well again. I feel better already."

"Oh, that's nice," Peter said politely.

"When we reach the Suez Canal the ship will travel as easily as if she were on a river, and I've never yet been seasick in the Mediterranean."

He watched to see what Peter would say. But Peter

remained silent, staring out over the water. He brooded thoughtfully: Suez Canal, Mediterranean — if he only knew how far off they were — if he decided to run away again he would have to do it before Mr. Peperkorn recovered completely.

"When we arrive in Alexandria I think everything will be over."

"Certainly!" Peter said, and meant something quite different from what Mr. Peperkorn meant. Alexandria — Alexandria! That might be his last chance.

That was the first day that Peter disobeyed the Captain. He had promised not to go down to the lower decks, and to avoid the coolies and the untouchables. When he was halfway down the iron stairs he suddenly remembered his promise, but his feet carried him further, through the dark passageways until he stood before a sliding door made of sheet iron. A great noise of voices came from behind the door, gossiping, laughing and singing, and suddenly a child screamed. Was it possible children were in there? Peter pushed the door open.

He was met by darkness, smells and people. Somewhere under the ceiling something golden appeared to be shining, and when his eyes got used to the dimness he recognized a tin Buddha, on whose fat stomach a gleam of sunshine had fallen. The Chinese were squatting under him. As Peter came in they raised their heads from their rice bowls and stared at him.

The Indians were sitting around in another corner, and they all stopped talking. One of them, a taller, bigger man than the others, got up and came toward him.

"Get out of here," he said. "You're a European, get out quick!"

"I'm not a European; I only look like one," Peter said in Hindustani. "Kanti is an untouchable and he's my friend, and Fu Ling's a Chinese and he's my brother."

The huge Indian was laughing now. "Get out just the same. I'll tell the others about you and you can come again when you aren't so well dressed."

And Peter put his hands on his forehead just as the Indians do and bowed his head in greeting. One or two of them laughed.

When he next returned he soon became their friend. The tall Indian always stood somewhere near him; he appeared to be one of their leaders; it was he who decided when they were to sleep, when they should eat or sing.

He told them all about Mahatma Gandhi, the great leader, who had made the lot of the untouchables easier, and who had wanted to bring them freedom. Peter listened, and trusted absolutely. He didn't notice the occasional dark glint in some of the Indians' eyes, or the yellow gleam in the eyes of the Chinese.

The leader stood between them and accepted the gifts of bananas, bread, canned milk and jams which Peter had taken from the Captain's table for them.

One day the Captain said, "I don't know why, boy, but

you're always so dirty these days. When you come into
my cabin you smell like the Chinese. It really is time that
Mr. Peperkorn got well."

After that Peter was careful. He didn't take quite so
much from the Captain's table, and the Captain wondered what had happened to his appetite.

A day or two later one of his sailor friends who was
washing the deck called out to him: "Can you see something over there?" He put his mop against the rails and
pointed.

"Land!" Peter shouted. "There are yellow hills and
palm trees. Is that Alexandria?"

"No, that's Arabia, and tonight we shall be level with
Aden, the English port on the Red Sea. Have you good
eyes? Can you see the shadow across the water over
there?"

"Ships!"

"British warships. And can you hear something? Look,
there they are!"

From far away, where the land lay, two jets with back-
swept wings approached. Their shadows raced across the
deck while Peter stared up at them, remembering for the
first time a snow-covered meadow, and high up in the sky
a screaming noise, the shadow of an airplane, a loud
cracking and a crunching. His Russian father was saying:
"The bridge is hit."

"They smash bridges with airplanes," Peter said. "I
was there; I saw how they smashed up Ten Middle Road!"

Now he knew — he knew something more about himself.

"Well, if you want to see more airplanes keep your eyes open today when we arrive off Aden," his friend the sailor told him.

Peter did keep his eyes open, but the first thing he saw was Mr. Peperkorn, who seemed to have recovered and had been looking for him.

"There you are! Now your lazing around is going to stop! The police are coming on board and they will examine all the passports. Among the rabble down below there's supposed to be an untouchable leader who has managed to get out of India; that's the man they're looking for. The Captain will have to hand him over if they find him."

The Hindu — his tall friend!

"They're not rabble —" Peter stuttered, but just in time remembered that he wasn't supposed to know anything about them.

The passengers formed a line and the police went along the row quickly, picking out one or two passports and handing them back again. They looked thoughtfully at a tall dark gentleman under a tropical helmet, missed Mr. Peperkorn and the elegant Edward who lounged in a bored way near his mother, and suddenly stopped in front of Peter — such a dirty fellow between the first-class passengers.

"Here's a little untouchable — I think we've got him!"

They were enjoying the joke but Mr. Peperkorn did not think it funny. He seized Peter's hand. "My son, Peter Peperkorn, twelve years old; here's his passport."

"Peter Reisiger, five years old, Ten Middle Road," said Peter at the same time, but as they couldn't understand German they didn't notice that father and son were contradicting each other. The police slapped Peter on the shoulder and laughed. "Well, he's a fine lad. A bit dirty — odd sort of father."

They went below decks. Peter waited anxiously, paying little attention to the scene around him. Then suddenly he saw that they had found their man. There he was! Peter bent low over the railings and watched the police coming up the gangway with his friend between them: the untouchable leader who had told him about Gandhi, about his fight for all those suppressed people, and how he had turned rebellion and chaos into order and peace.

"What are you shaking for? You look horrified!"

Peter looked at Mr. Peperkorn and tears of anger came into his eyes. He wanted to scream that the police were taking his best friend away, for he suddenly realized what the untouchable meant to him — freedom! He could have taken Peter with him when he left the ship at Alexandria. He could have done it, he could have —

Mr. Peperkorn was saying, "Really you can't cry about everything that happens in the world."

"Yes, I can," Peter roared, quite beside himself. "I'll cry when I want to, and I'll laugh when I want to too!"

"Then you'll do it in your cabin if you can't behave like civilized people!" And Peter disappeared into his cabin. But he didn't cry anymore, just stared in front of him with hard eyes. "Just have a bit more patience, bear," he comforted him and himself. "In Alexandria . . ."

23

Runaway on the Nile

THEY were going through the Suez Canal, and Peter was behaving very well.

"You've been so obedient these last few days," Mr. Peperkorn said, "that you deserve a reward. The ship will stop at Alexandria and I shall take you with me when I go ashore and show you something of Egypt."

"Well, if I have to," Peter said slowly. "I've already seen so many countries!"

"Then you'll see one more," the Dutchman said angrily, "there's still plenty for you to learn."

Peter's thoughts chased each other around in his head. Was it going to be as easy as that? Alexandria! A voice inside him said: "You won't get home so quickly that way!" And another voice answered: "But it's not likely that he'll let you go home." The first voice said: "Mother has been waiting for you for so long." But the irresponsible voice replied: "A bit longer won't matter. She's got no idea that you're coming, and how do you know that at home they won't be just like Mr. Peperkorn?"

That was it. Mr. Peperkorn was not the only one to

blame for the fact that Peter had decided to remain in Alexandria. He was afraid of going home: the journey on the ship had made him realize how strange everything there would be. Just a little longer, another adventure, and then he would be willing to let them catch him. But not just yet!

They were sitting in the Semiramis bar in Alexandria, Peter and Mr. Peperkorn.

On the other side of the square there was a small mosque, with a high tower. A balcony ran around the top. A crowd of people began to gather in the little square, and suddenly a loud voice came out of the tower.

"Allah is great," the muezzin called from the minaret. "There is no other God than Allah and Mohammed is his Prophet. Come and pray."

Allah! Mohammed! Ibrahim's voice from the Kirghiz steppes sounded in Peter's ears; there too they prayed like this. Peter was suddenly white. He stood up shaking.

"I don't feel well. Mr. Peperkorn. May I go out, please?"

"The waiter will show you where it is," Mr. Peperkorn said, a little annoyed. But Peter was already at the door accompanied by laughing glances from the neighboring tables. Mr. Peperkorn hadn't noticed that Peter had carried the bear away with him.

The Mohammedans in front of the mosque had taken off their shoes and were kneeling on little carpets which they had brought with them. They had put their hands together and were deep in prayer. They took no notice of the boy with the moth-eaten bear in his arms who crept out of the door and came toward them.

He was soon lost among them, and just as they did, he bent his head down to the ground until his forehead touched it. They all lay there together, praying. Peter had never felt as close to God as he did at this moment — his fate would be decided in the next few moments.

When the Mohammedans got up so did he. The sky was suddenly red and a cold wind came from the sea nearby. Pressing close to the wall Peter slipped down a side street. He looked carefully around a corner and saw Mr. Peperkorn standing in the doorway of the hotel. The waiter was talking to him, and waving his big black hands to and fro. Mr. Peperkorn looked helplessly around. For a second Peter wavered, but then Edward appeared in the doorway too, and that settled it: Peter lost himself in the crowd.

"You were very nice to me, Mr. Peperkorn," he said to himself. "Thank you very much for everything. You were horrid and nice at the same time, but now —"

A feeling of freedom overcame him, and numbed the horrid fear he felt as the streets became narrower. The people disappeared into dirty houses, the short twilight began to fall, and suddenly a crowd of black-haired children in long untidy shirts were running behind him crying, *"Baksheesh, baksheesh!"*

He ran on and got rid of them, and then he stopped, out of breath. The street was dark; in one or two of the doorways men in white robes were sitting looking across at him with curious eyes. One of them stood up and came purposefully toward him. But Peter was already running — he must get out of here quickly! And it wasn't until the street ended, with a few houses on the left and some gardens on the right, that he dared to stop.

His heart beat fast and his thoughts were confused, but he wasn't the same silly little child who had gotten lost in the world seven years ago. He knew now that people were both good and bad, and that there were many dangers in the world.

"But I'll manage," he said to himself, "only I must think how."

He frowned and looked down at his long legs, held the bear more tightly under his arm; the pleasure of having escaped from Mr. Peperkorn was still greater than the fear which was creeping over him.

He said to his bear: "I think Edward would begin to cry now. Mr. Peperkorn must have gone back to the ship, and the Captain will know about it already, and he'll tell the radio. They found the untouchable, who had gone much further then I have; we'd better hide ourselves quickly so no one can see us. It's lucky that it's already dark."

He went slowly down the sandy road. He had to jump over a ditch and then felt grass under his feet. When he stopped under the shade of a tree the evening light shone on the fruit: oranges!

"We'll stay here," Peter said to his bear, with his mouth full. "The grass is warm, and we've got enough to eat, and no one is likely to see us."

And just as it is with the Gods which one has made oneself — the bear agreed with him.

The fellaheen boy Abdulla was walking behind his ox. It was very early in the morning and Abdulla cracked his whip happily. It was still cold because of the nearness of the desert. An hour or two later he would become tired under the hot rising sun, and when it was evening he would go to sleep over the onion soup which his mother would cook for him.

Like his father and his grandfather when they had been children, and all the other fellaheen boys for thousands of years, he had to look after the oxen until he was able to do heavier work. This ox was chained to a huge wooden wheel which disappeared into a well. Clay pots were hung on the wheel, and as it went around they were filled with water. At this moment Abdulla's mother lifted one of them and carried it away on her head. Her black clothes blew in the breeze.

"I'll water the onions near the little orange tree; it'll be hot today," she said.

Women were coming along the small path from a long way off. They lifted full pots from the wheel, replacing

them with empty ones, and went to their land on the
edge of the desert. Abdulla ran along behind his ox, and
thought that he would have preferred to go into town
where all the foreigners were. If there were no policeman
nearby one could shout *"Baksheesh, baksheesh,"* and
then one was able to bring a little money home in the
evening. If one was plucky enough one could get more.
Abdulla's family were very poor.

Suddenly his mother was standing beside him again
and with her was a stranger. Abdulla let go of the rope,
and the ox at once stood still and went to sleep. Abdulla
looked at the stranger; unfortunately he was only a boy;
he didn't look as if he had much money; it would be no
good begging from him.

"He was asleep under our orange tree, quite stiff from
the cold night air, and I had to shake him awake. Unfortunately he's eaten some of our oranges."

"Shall not the hungry eat?"

"I wanted to sell them in the town tomorrow; we need
the money."

"You'll get a good reward from his father for finding
him."

Abdulla and Peter stood and looked at each other. The
sun was beginning to warm Peter, and these seemed to
be friendly folk.

"He helped me water my onions, so he can't be a bad
person," the mother said, "but I can't understand a word

"*Father is standing beside me and says I've got to come to the point. He'll soon get leave and then we'll come to get you. That's much better than if you had to make the long journey alone, now that you've got both Father and Mother. He wanted to leave me here alone, but I can't allow that. You really must show me the Pyramids!*" . . .

"Oh, the Pyramids," Peter said, and quite understood that his mother was only joking. When people are very happy they like making jokes.

"*Please give our greetings to Herr Schmidt,*" Herr Schmidt read further. "*He's a good man. There are many good people in the world, my son, who've taken such care of you. Are you as grateful to them as I am? I really am very happy. Look after yourself, Peter — we'll soon meet. Your Mother.*

"*P.S. One more thing, Herr Schmidt must write your height and size. I want to knit you a pullover. When you arrive here it will be winter. — Your Mother.*"

"Always these P.S.'s," said Herr Schmidt.

Peter rose and went to the window. The sky was blood-red over the desert. The palm trees had turned dark; night was coming. When Peter turned around his face looked like that of a man.

"I can show them the Pyramids, can't I, Herr Schmidt?"

"Yes, you must do that," said Herr Schmidt, "but show her the bear straightaway. You had him at home!"

"Naturally," Peter said, and added slowly, "if you don't think he's too dirty for her."

"For a mother, certainly not."

"No, for my mother, of course not."

He was as happy as if he were already at home.